camp CONFIDENTIAL

Politically In Correct

GROSSET & DUNLAP
Published by the Penguin Group
Penguin Group (USA) Inc., 375 Hudson Street,
New York, New York 10014, USA
Penguin Group (Canada), 90 Eglinton Avenue East, Suite 700, Toronto,
Ontario M4P 2Y3, Canada (a division of Pearson Penguin Canada Inc.)
Penguin Books Ltd., 80 Strand, London WC2R 0RL, England
Penguin Group Ireland, 25 St. Stephen's Green, Dublin 2, Ireland
(a division of Penguin Books Ltd.)
Penguin Group (Australia), 250 Camberwell Road, Camberwell, Victoria
3124, Australia (a division of Pearson Australia Group Pty. Ltd.)
Penguin Books India Pvt. Ltd., 11 Community Centre,
Panchsheel Park, New Delhi—110 017, India
Penguin Group (NZ), 67 Apollo Drive, Rosedale, North Shore 0632,
New Zealand (a division of Pearson New Zealand Ltd.)
Penguin Books (South Africa) (Pty.) Ltd., 24 Sturdee Avenue,
Rosebank, Johannesburg 2196, South Africa
Penguin Books Ltd., Registered Offices: 80 Strand,
London WC2R 0RL, England

Penguin Books Ltd., Registered Offices:
80 Strand, London WC2R 0RL, England

Cover design by Ching N. Chan
Front cover images © David Toase/Photodisc/Getty Images, Inc.

Library of Congress Cataloging-in-Publication is available.

ISBN 978-0-448-45267-8   10 9 8 7 6 5 4 3 2 1

camp CONFIDENTIAL

Politically In Correct

by Melissa J. Morgan

Grosset & Dunlap
An Imprint of Penguin Group (USA) Inc.

PROLOGUE

Posted by: Natalie
Subject: Oh. My. GAWD!

Guys, you'll never guess who I just saw on *Nightly News*! (Brief sidebar—my mom thinks discussing current events after thirty minutes of Katie Couric will somehow prep me for when I take the SAT, like, a million years from now.) Our very own Dr. Steve! Apparently Camp Walla Walla is one of the first camps to "go green," and he is planning this amazing festival to open the summer season.

I know, some of you might be thinking, "Um . . . so what?" or "Natalie, do you have brain freeze again?" But wait . . . it gets better!!!

The president—as in the president of OUR COUNTRY—is sending his daughter, Tricia, to Camp Walla Walla for a week! Since he was billed as "the first green president" during his reelection campaign, he wants his daughter to participate in the festival. Isn't that INSANE?! And think about it—Tricia is our age, so we could be sharing a bunk with the daughter of the leader of the free world! I don't think I've been this excited about camp in the history of forever. Only two more days to go! =)

Ugh. Katie Couric just signed off and now my mom is preparing index cards. Ha! JK!

Anyway, I'll sign back on later. Bye!

PS: Can we convince Dr. Steve to get a stylist? His favorite hat looked pretty ratty on TV.

Posted by: Jenna
Subject: The prez's daughter? Fo realz?

Seriously?! The president's daughter is going to be at Camp Walla Walla?! You better not be pranking us, Nat. That's my job! Tee-hee.

Posted by: Chelsea
Subject: The reports are all true!

My parents saw the segment on the news, too! Every time I see Tricia on TV, she looks amazing. Great designer clothes. Flawless makeup. Precious mini Cavadoodle in her oversized purse. Love it!

Posted by: Sarah
Subject: Question

Do you think Tricia's bodyguard will have to share a bunk with us, too? That could be weird.

Posted by: Sloan
Subject: Facts about the First Daughter

I Googled Tricia and here's what I found out:
1) Her favorite food is seedless red grapes.
2) She speaks three languages.
3) The name of her Cavadoodle is Paris (after her favorite city in the world).
4) She does yoga three times a week.
Wow! I like her already. Can't wait to see all of you in a few days!

Posted by: Brynn
Subject: American Idol

Cavadoodle? Yoga? Speaks three languages? I'm impressed! Not too fond of red grapes, though. I mean, isn't everyone's favorite food pizza? Just sayin'.

Posted by: Natalie
Subject: Can't wait

Here's to another great year at camp! See you all on Sunday. Yippee!!!!

Posted by: Avery
Subject: Of all summers . . .

I can't believe my stepmother chose this one to have a baby. You know what else I can't believe? That I suddenly decided that it was important to do the right thing and chose to stay home and help her with it. I mean, with him. To help her with *him* I mean. So I hope you all enjoy your glamorous presidential summer without me and I'll think of you as I perfect my diapering skills.

Posted by: Natalie
Subject: Correction

Make that another great year that's going to be slightly less great now that Avery isn't coming . . .
Say it ain't so, Ave. I thought we had a good thing going, you and us Lakeview girls. You will be sorely missed.

chapter ONE

Late Sunday morning, Natalie Goode dumped two large, purple duffel bags on her camp-issued twin-size bed and wiped her glistening forehead with the back of her hand. Even though she was never big on working up a sweat, she couldn't have been happier to finally arrive at Camp Walla Walla. Not only was she going to see all of her best friends again, but she'd also have the opportunity to get to know the president of the United States's daughter at "The Greenest Camp in America."

There was truly nothing cooler than that.

"Only two bags this summer, Nat? You're definitely slipping."

Natalie had been a little gun-shy about smiling since she'd gotten her braces, but she couldn't stop herself from breaking into a toothy grin at the sound of that familiar voice. She spun around and saw Sloan, decked out in a pair of khaki shorts and a light green T-shirt.

"Shut up and give me a hug!" Natalie grabbed Sloan and wrapped her arms around her friend.

"Okay, okay. You're crushing me," Sloan said, her cheeks turning pink.

Natalie laughed and let go. "I'm sorry. I'm just excited to see you!"

"Sheesh. If that's how you say hello to me, I'm afraid of what you're going to do when our celebrity camper arrives," Sloan joked as she rolled her suitcase over to the bed adjacent to Natalie's.

"You're forgetting who you're talking to. Celebrities don't freak me out the way they do everyone else. They're just average people like you and me."

No one was a stranger to the fact that Natalie's father was mega–movie star Tad Maxwell, but sometimes Natalie felt the need to remind her friends that she wasn't a gossip-obsessed famemonger. One day she hoped not to be insecure about her Hollywood roots.

"How is it possible that I already got stung by a bee?"

Natalie and Sloan smiled in unison when they saw their friend Chelsea walking into the tent, holding her blond hair back and pointing at her neck. "Is it bad? Don't lie to me, I can take it."

"It's pretty standard for a bee sting, Chelse. Just red and puffy," Sloan answered.

"Well I can't let the president's daughter see me this way. She'll think I'm a complete loser," Chelsea said with a sigh.

"Oh stop it. You look great!" Natalie flung her arms around Chelsea and pulled her in close for a hug. "I've missed you!"

Chelsea stared over Natalie's shoulder at Sloan, confused. "Why is Natalie trying to squeeze me to death?"

"I haven't figured that out yet," Sloan replied, giggling.

"I'm just psyched to be here, that's all! Dr. Steve said on TV that the camp has a lot of cool new features, and this festival he mentioned sounds awesome, and there's a chance that the president's daughter will be staying in our bunk, and maybe there will be a lot of new boys this year." Natalie paused for a second to catch her breath. "I'm rambling, aren't I?"

"Yes, you are. Now release me from your choke hold so I can breathe," Chelsea croaked.

Natalie chuckled as Chelsea wiggled out of their embrace. "I can't wait to see everyone at orientation."

Sloan glanced at her watch. "Won't be long now. Dr. Steve's expecting us all at the new rotunda building at noon."

"I heard it's powered by solar panels on the roof," Natalie said.

"Do they still have calamine lotion at the infirmary? Because I am in desperate need of some," Chelsea said, scratching at her neck.

"If they do, I bet it's organic," Sloan said, smirking.

▲ ▲ ▲

Natalie was buzzing with such excitement that she couldn't sit still at the orientation meeting.

She was surrounded by more of her good friends—Jenna, Priya, Brynn, Joanna, and Sarah, who were all in her bunk this summer—and the new rotunda building was absolutely amazing. The solar panels on the ceiling were made of a translucent material, so everyone could look up and gaze at the white, puffy clouds that were moving slowly through the perfectly blue sky.

"I wish Dr. Steve would get on with the show. We have so much catching up to do," said Priya.

"Never mind catching up! Has anyone seen Tricia yet?" Chelsea said, her head pivoting back and forth as she checked out the crowd.

"Nope, not me," replied Sarah.

"I haven't, either," Brynn chimed in.

"Maybe she's in disguise!" Priya suggested.

Natalie giggled with the rest of the girls.

Priya crossed her arms over her chest. "Don't laugh. I saw it in a movie once."

"Whoa, check out the eye candy over there," Joanna said, pointing to a spot a few rows ahead of them.

Natalie peered over the heads of the group in front of her and glanced at a posse of boys sitting to the left of them. A very good-looking, brown-haired, olive-skinned boy who she had never seen before was talking with David, Connor, and Jordan.

"Okay, I have to say it," Sloan said with a wide grin. "Yuuuuum!"

Just as Natalie and the other girls burst out laughing, Dr. Steve stepped in front of the podium and tapped the microphone a few times to make sure it was on. Then he cleared his throat, causing some feedback to echo throughout the room. Natalie covered her ears and winced.

Well, that's one way to get everyone's attention.

"Sorry! Didn't mean for that to happen," Dr. Steve said in a flustered manner. He nervously ran his fingers through his hair and took a deep breath. "What I meant to say was, welcome back to Camp Walla Walla, folks!"

Natalie clapped cheerfully with the rest of the campers as she scanned the crowd a bit more for familiar faces.

"As one of the greenest camps in America, we are fully equipped to conserve energy by using only natural resources," Dr. Steve said to the crowd of campers who were all listening intently. "That being said, we're going to have to implement a few changes to our way of life here, which might take some getting used to."

"I don't like the sound of this," Chelsea mumbled under her breath.

Dr. Steve continued. "First of all, we are going to start composting our waste so we can fertilize the soil here naturally. That means there will probably be more slugs and worms hanging around, but don't worry. They're an important part of the biodegradable machine!"

"Ew, gross!" Brynn said.

"We'll also be strictly monitoring our water use. Everyone here will only have three minutes to take a shower," Dr. Steve added.

Natalie's eyes widened. *Three minutes?! It takes me that long just to condition my hair!*

"And we're also going to grow a lot of our own produce in our beautiful new vegetable garden," Dr. Steve continued.

"All these things are great, but when is he going to talk about Tricia?" Priya whispered into Natalie's ear.

"Hopefully soon," Natalie whispered back. While Natalie thought the vegetable garden sounded pretty cool, some of the other changes at camp weren't sounding so good, especially the shower thing.

Dr. Steve went on. "I'm sure you will all be happy to hear that we've modified the no computer rule here at camp. We realize that allowing you folks to communicate with your family and friends at home via e-mail will cut down on the use of paper, and a generous parent donated one PC that everyone can share. Isn't that great?"

Natalie sighed underneath her breath. *"One PC? Well, that works for me, but what's everyone else going to use?"*

Dr. Steve took a deep breath into the microphone. "I'm also sure the word has spread that the president's daughter, Tricia, is visiting Camp Walla Walla for a whole week," he announced.

At this, all the campers erupted into wild applause. Some girls even jumped out of their chairs, shrieking like crazed fans.

"All right, settle down," Dr. Steve said with

a chuckle. "I hate to disappoint you, but Tricia is in Vienna with her parents, so she won't be here until Thursday."

The shrieking girls immediately groaned and sat back down in disappointment.

"We're all thrilled that she is coming here to spend time with us and speak at the Green Festival, which is an event that we're holding next Saturday and Sunday in celebration of our new green initiative. And here to tell you about that is one of our new counselors, Jasmine."

Dr. Steve stepped away from the podium to let a tall young woman with cocoa-colored skin and brown eyes approach the microphone.

Jasmine leaned into the microphone. "Hi, campers. I'm super-excited to be here, and I'm especially excited to help with the Green Festival. In a nutshell, the festival is all about honoring nature, and there's no better way to do that than by asking our local community to join us here for two days of organic food, games, and all sorts of family fun."

Natalie turned to Sloan and saw a wide smile form on her friend's face. This was just the kind of New Agey thing that Sloan lived for.

"Of course, there will be a lot of planning involved, so Dr. Steve and I are forming a committee to oversee the event. And the committee will need a chairperson to lead them in the right direction."

Now it was Natalie's turn to break into a big, cheesy grin. Even though her mom was a little zany for wanting to prep Natalie for college super early,

Natalie couldn't help but think that this chairperson gig would make her extra desirable to universities down the road. Maybe if she did this job really well, all the Ivy League schools would come knocking at her door. And it didn't exactly hurt that Nat's mom had promised her a brand-new iPod touch when she got back if she did anything college-application worthy while she was away.

Truth be told, Natalie imagined that when the time came, people would assume that she could get into any college she wanted because her father was the famous Tad Maxwell. Natalie was never comfortable with people thinking that she had it so easy. Which was why it was important for her achievements to be her own. This chairperson gig seemed like just the thing.

"Dr. Steve and I have no doubt there will be a lot of interest in the chairperson position, so we'd like those of you who want to be considered to write an essay on what 'going green' means to you. The camper with the best essay will get the spot," Jasmine explained.

Natalie's smile vanished instantly.

Me? Write an essay?

She could feel her face growing hot and her palms getting sticky. While she consistently maintained an A average, written expression had always been her one trouble spot. So much for Green Festival Chairperson.

"Good luck, everyone," Jasmine said before switching places again with Dr. Steve.

Yeah, luck isn't going to help me, Natalie thought, her hopes of Ivy League colleges and new technology dwindling in her mind.

"That pretty much covers the big announcements," Dr. Steve said when he returned to the podium. "Now let's start having an unforgettable summer!"

Chelsea hated rainy days at camp, especially early in the season. Thankfully, her friends knew exactly how to turn a Monday afternoon rest period indoors into a Friday night slumber party. Jenna had hooked up her MP3 player to some minispeakers and Natalie had dumped the contents of her overstuffed duffel bags in the center of the room so all of the girls could try her clothes on.

"I wish Tricia were here to see how much fun we can all be," Brynn said as she applied some of Natalie's fire—engine red lip gloss to her lips.

"Tricia's in Vienna, Brynn. Camp Walla Walla is cool and all, but I'm sure it's going to seem rather hokey to someone as sophisticated as she is," Joanna answered.

Jenna let out a huff. "You're making her sound like a snob. She probably likes the same things we do."

"I'm with Jenna. I bet Tricia is really down-to-earth and nice," Chelsea agreed.

Chelsea hoped she and Jenna were right. Just because Tricia was worldly and smart didn't mean she wouldn't be as sweet and friendly as she was in TV interviews. In fact, Chelsea had started to really look up to Tricia, especially after reading an interview she did in *Gloss Magazine*. Chelsea loved how Tricia seemed kind of glitzy like a supermodel, yet on the inside she was totally a normal girl. It turned out, Tricia never felt as if she had a real best friend. Chelsea could definitely relate to that, even if she would never admit it to the other girls. From that amazing interview alone, Chelsea could tell Tricia was a really great girl—one she would love to be true friends with.

"But what if she doesn't like us?" Sarah asked.

"God, that would be horrible," Brynn replied.

Chelsea felt a quick chill sprint up her spine. The thought of Tricia thinking she was a dork or something bothered her a lot. In all honesty, Chelsea saw how tight some of the other girls were, and she often wished she had someone who totally understood her. Chelsea knew she might be silly for thinking this, but she was starting to hope maybe Tricia could be that person.

"Guys, could you keep it down for a few minutes? I'm trying to get this essay finished." Sloan was sprawled out on her bed, flat on her stomach, scribbling in a three-subject notebook.

"Give it a rest, Sloan! You've been working on that thing for hours. I'm sure it's great," Priya said as she rubbed some coconut-vanilla lotion onto her elbows.

Sloan didn't take her eyes off her paper. "Thanks, Pree. But I just want to make sure it's perfect."

Chelsea shook her head. While the Green

Festival did sound like it was going to be a great time, she didn't really see it as something worth stressing over. Though she definitely appreciated some of the really cool changes at Camp Walla Walla, like how pretty she and her friends looked in the tents' new soft lighting, courtesy of eco-friendly, low-watt bulbs.

Still, was any of that going to matter when Tricia came to camp? Chelsea didn't think so.

"Well, I admire your dedication, Sloan," Sarah said as she tuned down the music. "I thought about writing an essay, but isn't camp supposed to be about fun, not homework?"

"I couldn't agree with you more," Chelsea chimed in. "I spent all year writing papers and taking tests."

Priya pulled a sleeveless, cobalt blue top out of the clothing pile and put it on over her white tank. "I already wrote my essay. It only took me twenty minutes."

Chelsea was about to poke fun at Priya's work ethic when her eyes zoomed in on the shirt her bunkmate was wearing. Chelsea couldn't believe her eyes—she'd seen it before. Tricia had worn the same shirt during the Oprah special! Who could forget that bejeweled neckline and the beautiful blue silk? Not Chelsea!

"Oh my God, Nat. Where did you get this?" Chelsea asked as Priya admired herself in a mirror. Chelsea had to bite her lip to keep from squealing like those frenzied girls from yesterday morning. If her bunkmates knew how much she idolized Tricia, they would definitely make fun of her.

When Natalie didn't answer, Chelsea spun around and saw her friend sitting cross-legged on her bed, peering out the window at the pouring rain. Natalie had been moping around like this ever since yesterday's orientation meeting. In the beginning she had seemed so excited about the festival and Tricia, but now it was like she was a total zombie.

"Hey, are you okay?" Chelsea forgot about her excitement over Tricia and the shirt and sat beside her friend, waiting for her to speak up.

"Yeah, I'm fine," Natalie finally answered in a weak voice.

Chelsea looked at Natalie skeptically. "I'm finding that a little hard to believe, Nat. You've been in such a weird mood lately."

Before Natalie could answer, Sarah tapped Chelsea on the shoulder. "Time to brave the storm and run to the dining hall, campers."

Chelsea glanced back at Natalie, who was still staring out the window. She looked like food was the last thing on her mind. "You guys go ahead. We'll be right behind you."

Everyone grabbed their rain ponchos and boots and scurried out of the tent in one big, squealing cluster. Everyone except for Chelsea and Natalie.

"The coast is clear. Now tell me what's up," Chelsea asked again. Normally she wasn't this pushy when it came to her bunkmates, but she could tell that something was bothering Natalie, and Chelsea's curiosity was getting the best of her.

Natalie turned to look at Chelsea, her lips curled into a pout. "It's the essay."

Geez, again with the essay? Why are Sloan and Nat even sweating this?

"What about it?"

"I tried to write one, like three or four times, but they were all terrible," Natalie whimpered.

"I'm sure they weren't that bad," Chelsea said, trying to reassure her.

"Ugh, and I was so excited about being the leader of the festival committee. It would be such a great thing to add to my extracurricular record," Natalie said as she pounded a fist into her pillow. "And then Dr. Steve had to turn it into a writing competition. I mean, since when does writing an essay have anything to do with planning a festival?"

"Well, maybe you should come up with an outline first and then write the essay based off that. I learned how to do it in English class this year and got an A on almost every paper," Chelsea suggested.

"Really?" Natalie asked hopefully.

"Yup! So why don't you start with an outline, and give this essay another shot?" Chelsea asked.

Natalie slouched her shoulders in defeat. "Because I won't be able to get it done in time. The essay has to be turned in by tomorrow night, and I'm such a slow writer to begin with."

Chelsea thought a moment, and then took a quick breath. She had the perfect solution! "Wait a sec. What if I wrote the essay for you?"

Natalie chewed her bottom lip nervously.

"Um . . . I don't know if I'm comfortable with cheating."

"It won't be cheating. I could interview you and then piece it all together, kind of like what a ghostwriter does," Chelsea suggested.

"Huh. Maybe you're right. But don't ghostwriters usually get paid or something?" Natalie asked.

"Well," Chelsea said, grinning. "You could always pay me with that blue shirt of yours. What do you think? Pleeeeeease?"

Natalie giggled. "Wow, Chelse, I don't think I've ever seen you beg before. Why do you want the shirt so badly?"

Chelsea took a deep breath. A voice inside her head told her not to admit the truth—that she wanted the shirt to impress Tricia. Natalie would definitely think she was lame and immature, especially since her father was a gigantic movie star with tons of his own obsessed followers. But she couldn't think of a cover fast enough.

"Promise not to laugh?" she asked hoping that the truth would at least earn her some leniency.

"Promise," Natalie said.

Chelsea cleared her throat and said, "Well, that shirt . . . it's the same one that Tricia wore in her Oprah interview."

A smile crept across Natalie's face. "Oh. Really?"

"Fine, go ahead and laugh," Chelsea said, rolling her eyes.

"I'm sorry, Chelse! I just didn't know you were such a diehard fan. Plus, the way you were talking about this shirt made me think it was something much more serious," Natalie said through a chuckle.

"Well, I am a diehard fan, and you can guess why I didn't tell anybody until now," Chelsea said, annoyed.

"I won't say a word, I swear." Natalie used her index finger to make an X over her heart.

"Good, and I won't tell anyone about our little arrangement, either."

"Okay, it's a deal," Natalie said, sticking her hand out for Chelsea to shake. Once Chelsea grabbed hold of it, Natalie added, "Thanks, Chelse. I really hope this works."

"Of course it'll work," Chelsea said confidently. "Just wait and see."

▲ ▲ ▲

Late that night, Chelsea and Natalie ducked out of their bunk and hid in the sports shack to work on Natalie's essay. Chelsea typed away on her laptop computer while Natalie talked about her thoughts on the environment, and why she wanted to be chairperson of the Green Committee.

"I'm getting some really great stuff here, Nat. It's a good thing I snuck my laptop into camp this year," Chelsea said as she batted at the keyboard.

"True, but at least now we have access to a computer. One we didn't have to sneak in, I mean," Natalie joked.

"Can you imagine having to share one computer with a hundred other campers, though? No one will ever get more than a few minutes to use it. Having a computer is really helping this interview go a lot faster—I can't imagine writing out all your answers by hand," Chelsea replied.

"That's true." Natalie paused and peered over Chelsea's shoulder to read what she had just written. "Hmm, I don't know if I like the idea of talking about my dad in this essay."

"What do you mean? I think that's the most interesting thing about you."

"Gee, thanks, Chelse!" Natalie spat.

"Don't get all offended. I'm just saying, people want to read about that stuff." Chelsea didn't understand why Natalie was getting all upset. All she was trying to do was help Natalie get what she wanted.

"I'm sure they do. But the reason I want to be chairperson is so I can get into college on my own terms, not just because I'm Tad Maxwell's daughter," Natalie explained.

Chelsea was confused. Wasn't college eons away?

"Nat, I think you worry too much about what other people think of you," Chelsea said.

"Everyone does, even you, Chelse," Natalie said firmly.

Chelsea knew Natalie had a point. Judging Natalie for being self-conscious was kind of hypocritical.

"Well, what if we include something in the essay that shows how your dad has used his celebrity for a good purpose," Chelsea suggested. Perhaps Natalie would feel more comfortable with that.

"Oooh, I like it," Natalie said, her mood instantly lifting.

"Can you think of anything that might be good?" Chelsea asked.

"Actually, I think so. It's about my dad and the San Diego Zoo," Natalie said.

"Wow, jackpot! People love animals just as much as they love movie stars," Chelsea said, smiling.

"You crack me up, Chelse," Natalie said. "Tricia is going to love your sense of humor."

Chelsea smiled even more. "You really think so?"

"Most definitely."

"Well, let's get back to work. I've got a lot of notes to take and you still have to rewrite all this stuff by hand," Chelsea said.

"Okay, let's do it," Natalie said, her voice filled with enthusiasm.

Chelsea was excited, too. This was going to be the best summer yet. She could feel it.

What Going Green Means to Me
by Natalie Goode

"Give me the splendid silent sun with all his beams full-dazzling."—Walt Whitman

When I was little, my dad used to take me to the San Diego Zoo on

Sundays. Sometimes enthusiastic fans would follow us around, hoping to get my father's autograph and maybe, if they were lucky, pictures with him near the lion's den. Other times we went unnoticed and unbothered in the crowds, snaking through the Wild Animal Park, where it felt like we had been transported to Africa.

My father was always gracious on those days when we were approached by people who had seen his movies, but to be honest, it always bothered me—not because we were being interrupted, but because they seemed to be missing the whole point of being there: to appreciate the beauty of the animals. Instead, it seemed to me that they were more impressed with seeing a star they had watched on the silver screen.

When I opened up to my dad and told

him how I felt, he decided that from then on he was going to use his high-profile status to bring awareness to a cause that meant a lot to him—the conservation of animals. Each time we went to the zoo and my father was asked for an autograph or photo, he would talk to his fans about the important work that was being done there. As for myself, I would hand out pamphlets that were issued by the zoo, which explained how people could get involved and support the organization by becoming a Zoological Society Member.

Our unique outreach program became quite popular, so the San Diego Zoo coordinated a celebrity charity auction. My father was the emcee and auctioneer, and I helped out behind the scenes, labeling all the items up for bid. It was such a great experience—I had fun and was able to lend a hand to the zoo, a place that I always loved to visit.

In my opinion, "going green" means getting involved in a cause that's special to you and educating others about it. This way, more people can spread the word, and before you know it, there is a whole community to support you and champion your beliefs. It can't be done in one day, but it can be done over time. All it takes is one dedicated individual to recruit a team and for that team to make a difference.

chapter

THREE

On Tuesday morning, the rain had cleared, the sun was shining, and it was hot enough for relays in the lake. But Sloan had another activity in mind. Dressed in a purple tankini and a wrap tied around her waist, Sloan grabbed her three-subject notebook and a pencil out of her tote bag, then snuck off in search of a good place to work on her essay. She chose a huge oak tree close to the water so she would be in earshot if someone called for her turn.

Just a few more finishing touches and I'll be done, Sloan thought as she sat down in the grass and opened up her notebook. All that was left to do was write a great closing line that would knock Dr. Steve's socks off. Sloan was really pleased with what she'd written and felt as though she had a pretty good chance of winning the committee chairperson's spot with it. Sloan had always been pro-environment, and she had grown up in an eco-friendly house, too. The Green Festival was so in line with her principles and interests, more than any other camp event in the past. She really wanted to be a part of it in a big way.

Sloan jerked her head up when she heard a big splash from the lake. She smiled when she spotted Natalie and Chelsea laughing hysterically during their leg of the relay. It looked like Chelsea had done one giant belly flop when she dove into the water after Natalie. Sloan was happy to see Natalie having a good time after being so bummed the day before. Sloan felt a twinge of guilt when she thought about how preoccupied she'd been—she hadn't even asked Natalie what was wrong.

However, that wave of negativity subsided the moment a tall, brown-haired, blue-eyed boy stepped into view. Actually, the same brown-haired boy that she'd "yummed" over at orientation the other day.

"Shouldn't you be dog-paddling with the rest of us?" the boy asked with an adorable smile.

Sloan blinked twice in disbelief. *Is he actually talking to me?*

"I'm just squeezing in a little study time between relays," she replied.

The boy chuckled a bit. "It's summer. Shouldn't study time be over?"

Great move, Sloan. Now he thinks you're a big freak!

"I'm just working on that essay—"

"For the Green Festival." The boy finished Sloan's sentence and sat down next to her. "We had an event like that at my old school in Alaska."

"Whoa—you're from Alaska?" Sloan said with surprise. She'd never met anyone from that far away before.

"I'm part Inuit, actually," he said, pointing to his slightly almond-shaped eyes.

Sloan blushed when she stared into them deeply. "That's really cool."

"So, can I take a peek at your essay?" he asked.

Sloan's heart filled with both excitement and dread. She was thrilled the adorable Alaskan boy was interested in her at all, but the thought of him going through her notebook made her uneasy. She also wasn't used to boys being this forward, but who really cared? He was SO cute!

"Um, I feel kind of funny about showing my writing to you when I don't even know your name."

"I'm Miles," the boy said. "It's nice to meet you, Sloan."

Sloan's breath caught in her throat. "Wait, how did you—"

"I saw you during orientation and I asked David who you were." Miles grinned. "Does that make me a creep?"

"No, it's cute," Sloan said, laughing.

Miles's cheeks flushed a little. "So now can I look at your essay? I promise I won't tell anyone what it says."

Sloan giggled. She liked how inquisitive and assertive Miles was.

"Sure," Sloan said as she handed Miles her note-book. "It's not finished, though. I still have to write a snappy closing line."

Miles nodded his head and began reading right away. Sloan could feel her stomach churning with anxiety. She thought her essay was great, but she'd never intended to have anyone read it but Dr. Steve, and maybe Jasmine.

Miles closed Sloan's notebook when he was finished reading and handed it back to her. "So, where are you from?"

Sloan gave Miles a bewildered look. Didn't he have anything to say about her essay? "Um . . . Arizona."

"Cool. I've been there. I really like it," Miles said.

"Uh . . . that's nice," Sloan replied. "What did you think of my essay?"

Miles pulled up some grass from the roots and sprinkled it in front of his feet. "It was . . . okay."

Okay?! Sloan thought. *It was better than okay, wasn't it?!*

"Don't you think that's a little vague?" Sloan asked.

"I'm sorry," Miles muttered. "Never mind. It was good."

"No, tell me what you were going to say," Sloan insisted. "I can take it."

"Well . . . um . . . I just thought that it was a little . . ."

"What?"

"Um . . . you just don't seem so excited is all," Miles said through a cough. "I'm sorry, Sloan. All your facts are great, but I don't get the feeling from reading the essay that you're so into it."

Sloan's face went speeding-comet hot.

Adorable or not, Sloan was no longer happy about sharing Miles's company.

"I think I hear my counselor Ellie calling me, so I'd better go." Sloan got up abruptly and tucked her notebook under her arm.

The smile on Miles's face vanished as he stood up and shoved his hands into the pockets of his swim trunks. Obviously he knew that his remarks had hurt Sloan's feelings.

"Okay," he murmured, his eyes cast down at the ground.

"See ya," Sloan mumbled, trying hard not to cry as she made her way back to her friends.

▲   ▲   ▲

The next day, Sloan and the rest of Camp Walla Walla gathered together for a picnic lunch at the main promenade, where Dr. Steve was going to announce the Green Festival committee chairperson. Sloan solemnly pushed her free-range chicken salad around on her recycled paper plate and prepared herself for the worst. Even though in the end she was so confident in her writing that she'd turned in her essay without making any changes to it, she couldn't get Miles's "not so exciting" comment out of her head.

"Are you feeling sick or something?" Chelsea asked. "You haven't touched any of your food."

"I guess I'm just not hungry," Sloan mumbled.

"Aha," Brynn said with a mischievous smirk. "Then the prognosis is lovesickness."

Sloan was not amused. Teasing from her friends

was not what she needed right now. "Stop it, guys. I'm not in the mood."

"But are you in the mood for loooove?" Jenna cooed.

"I mean it, Jenna," Sloan said sharply.

"Don't get mad, Sloan," Priya said. "We just couldn't help but notice you and that new guy chatting it up yesterday by the lake. You guys looked rather cozy."

"Oh. Him," Sloan said flatly.

"What's his story, Sloan? We're dying to know," Joanna said after taking a sip of organic root beer.

But before Sloan could tell her friends about her awkward encounter with Miles, Dr. Steve appeared at the corner of the promenade with a bullhorn and commanded everyone's attention with a booming voice.

"Good afternoon, campers! I hope you are enjoying the delicious picnic lunch and the neat aluminum water bottles that we'll be using all summer."

"Could Dr. Steve be any louder?" Chelsea asked, plugging her ears.

"I think everyone in the state can hear him!" Sarah added.

"Well, I won't keep you all in suspense any longer," Dr. Steve continued. "The winner of the 'What Going Green Means to Me' essay contest has been decided, and before I announce who that is, I just want to thank all the campers who entered for all their hard work and enthusiasm."

Sloan felt a wave of nervousness ripple through

her body. This was the moment she had been waiting for. She almost couldn't bear to listen.

"Congratulations to Natalie Goode! You are the Green Festival committee chairperson!"

Sloan slumped forward when she heard the news, but tried not to look too disappointed for her friend's sake. Natalie, on the other hand, shrieked as though she'd just won the lottery.

"Way to go, Nat!" Sarah cheered and hugged Natalie.

"Thank you so much," Natalie gushed. "I'm so psyched!"

"Me too," Chelsea said, smiling.

Sloan knew she should congratulate Natalie, but she was having such a hard time keeping her emotions in check. In fact, her throat suddenly felt raw and she doubted that she could say anything at all.

"I'm so proud of you, Natalie," Dr. Steve said as he popped up at their table.

Natalie was glowing with happiness. "Thanks, Dr. Steve. I'm really excited about helping you and Jasmine plan the Green Festival. I already have a bunch of ideas written down."

"Great, I can't wait to hear them," Dr. Steve replied, smiling. Then he turned to Sloan and put his hand on her shoulder. "Sloan, I can see that you're disappointed."

Sloan gulped. *Is it that obvious?*

"I just want you to know that your essay was good. You just didn't seem all that passionate."

Sloan swallowed hard. Maybe Miles had

been right about her essay. And sure, her feelings had been hurt, but why hadn't she taken his opinion seriously? Perhaps she could have rewritten it and won. Maybe her reaction to his comment *was* a little overdramatic. Maybe she just hadn't given Miles enough of a chance.

"Natalie, meet me and Jasmine in my office tomorrow at nine AM so we can start getting organized," Dr. Steve said. "The president's daughter arrives tomorrow afternoon. There's a lot to be done!"

"You bet," Natalie replied enthusiastically.

Once Dr. Steve wandered off, Sloan managed to choke back her heartbreak long enough to approach Natalie. She took a deep breath and reminded herself that being a sore loser didn't do anyone any good.

"Nice job, Natalie," Sloan said, her voice trembling a little. "I'm sure you're going to be an amazing chairperson."

"Thanks, Sloan. I really hope you'll volunteer to be in the group. It's going to be so much fun, I promise," Natalie said brightly.

Sloan half smiled. "Of course I will."

"Cool! Now let's get ready for Tricia!" Natalie said, throwing her arms in the air.

Sloan let out a heavy sigh and wondered if she could be any more jealous of Natalie than she was right now.

chapter

FOUR

On Thursday morning, Natalie was actually whistling in the shower. That's how overjoyed she was about winning the essay contest. In just a short while, she was going to be meeting with Dr. Steve and coordinating all these incredible plans for the festival. As Natalie lathered her hair with shampoo, she imagined her future college interview. She would wear her cutest preppy outfit, of course, and the admissions director would be incredibly impressed with the activities portion of her application. Now she had something besides the notoriety of her father's name to make her record stand out from the crowd.

Natalie was just rinsing the shampoo out of her hair when she heard a loud beep. Next thing she knew, the water in her shower stall suddenly stopped running.

"Hey! What happened?" Natalie cried out to no one in particular.

"Looks like Dr. Steve is taking this water conservation thing really seriously, because the showers have built-in timers," a voice replied from outside Natalie's shower stall. "Apparently nobody could abide by the three-minute rule!"

Natalie wiped some suds off her forehead. "Chelsea? Is that you?"

"The one and only!" she chirped.

"Is there any way to reset the timer? I still have to rinse my hair."

"I don't think so," Chelsea replied. "Hold on, let me fill up a cup with some water from the sink."

"Thanks, Chelse. I owe you one!" Natalie said, relieved.

Actually, when Natalie thought about it, she owed Chelsea a lot these days. Natalie had wanted to thank Chelsea in private for writing her essay, but hadn't gotten the chance to. Maybe now was a good opportunity.

A knock on the shower stall jarred Natalie out of her thoughts.

"Here you go," Chelsea said, sliding a cup filled with water underneath the stall door.

"You rock, Chelse!" Natalie said. "Hey, is there anyone else in here?"

"Yeah, Joanna just walked in," Chelsea said in a soft voice.

Natalie would have to tell Chelsea how much she appreciated her help some other time. Even though she didn't feel like teaming up with Chelsea to write the essay was wrong, Natalie wasn't exactly comfortable with that information being common knowledge. Sure, the story about her dad and the zoo was completely true, but Chelsea had put it into her own words, and Natalie knew that wasn't the same as writing it herself.

"Okay. Well, I'll talk to you later."

"All right. See ya," Chelsea said, clicking the bathroom door shut behind her on the way out.

Natalie poured the water over her head and dried off with her big, fluffy towel in a flash. She dressed in record time and sprinted across the campgrounds. She was practically out of breath when she arrived at Dr. Steve's office.

The door was open a crack, so Natalie popped her head in. However, much to her surprise, Sloan was sitting in one of the chairs opposite Dr. Steve's desk.

What is she doing here? Natalie thought.

"Hey, Natalie. Glad you could make it. Why don't you have a seat?" Dr. Steve gestured to the chair next to Sloan.

"Um . . . okay," Natalie said warily. What was going on here? Weren't she and Dr. Steve supposed to be meeting about the Green Festival?

"I asked Sloan to join us for a reason, Natalie," Dr. Steve began. "You see, I spoke with Jasmine and some of the other counselors last night and everyone feels that, while you would make an excellent chairperson for the committee, there's a different task for which you are more uniquely suited."

Natalie squinted at Dr. Steve, completely confused. What could be more important than being chairperson of the festival committee? "I don't understand, Dr. Steve."

"Since Tricia will be unfamiliar with the camp

and what we do here, we felt that she might need someone to show her around for the first couple of days," he explained.

Natalie couldn't stop her eyelids from twitching. "ME?!"

"Of course! We think you'd be able to relate to each other very well, especially since you know how uncomfortable it can be to have all eyes on you because you have a famous father," Dr. Steve replied.

Natalie raised her eyebrows in acknowledgement. She had never thought of that before.

"Listen, the choice is yours. If you want to stay on board as chairperson, that's fine. But if you're okay with being Tricia's go-to person, Sloan is ready and excited to step in as head of the committee," Dr. Steve said, nodding in Sloan's direction.

Natalie glanced at Sloan, who seemed as though she were hoping Natalie would say yes to Dr. Steve's proposal. Although Natalie wanted to deny it, Sloan was just as eager to be group chairperson as Natalie, and she knew Sloan would do a great job.

The only thing was, Natalie had wanted this position to bolster her college apps. Showing the president's daughter around probably wouldn't serve that purpose. And if Natalie tried to cash in on her experience as Tricia's guide somewhere down the road, wouldn't that be kind of hypocritical? After all, Natalie constantly worried that people only liked her for her famous father.

But Natalie couldn't ignore what Dr. Steve had said. He was right about her being in the same position as Tricia. It wasn't too long ago that Natalie had been hoping no one at camp would find out about her movie star father. If she'd had someone like Tricia around back then, maybe Natalie would have felt more at ease about making new friends and being herself. That's what camp was all about—friendship, not prepping for college.

That settled it. Giving up her chairperson spot was obviously Natalie's patriotic duty. Besides, Sloan looked so devastated yesterday when she found out she didn't win the essay contest. This would really perk her friend up.

"Okay, Dr. Steve. I'll help out with Tricia," Natalie said with a chipper smile.

"That's great, Natalie. I really appreciate your flexibility," Dr. Steve replied.

"I promise to take good care of the committee, Nat," Sloan said as a wide grin spread across her face.

A twinge of jealousy tweaked at Natalie's heart, but she did her best to ignore it. "I know you'll do an awesome job, Sloan."

"Wonderful, girls. Well, I'm heading out to meet Tricia and her security people at the train station at one o'clock. Would you like to join me, Natalie?" Dr. Steve asked.

Whatever smidge of jealousy Natalie had felt evaporated in an instant. She was going to meet the president's daughter! That was a pretty decent trade-off.

"I'd love to go!" Natalie said, hoping Tricia would be exactly how she'd imagined.

▲ ▲ ▲

A few hours later, Natalie stood next to Dr. Steve and watched as Tricia disembarked the train, carrying a designer tote bag in one hand and an animal carrier in the other. She was surrounded by three gigantic men in dark navy suits and aviator sunglasses holding push-to-talk phones in their hands.

Although these guys were definitely intimidating, Natalie couldn't take her eyes off of Tricia. She looked even better in person than she did on TV! Her long, chestnut hair was shinier and bouncier; her clothes were trendier; even her teeth were whiter. Natalie looked down at herself and suppressed a groan. What had possessed her to wear sandals and shorts?! Sure it was hot and humid outside, but now was the time to be fashionable, not comfortable!

"You must be Dr. Steve," Tricia said with an outstretched hand that happened to have a perfect French manicure.

"It's such a pleasure to meet you, miss," Dr. Steve said as he shook Tricia's hand. "We are so thrilled to have you at Camp Walla Walla as we put together our very first Green Festival."

"Oh, the pleasure is all mine," Tricia said, her hazel eyes glittering. "And thanks for picking us up at the train station. I would have come in a car, but I get really bad motion sickness."

"Not a problem at all," Dr. Steve reassured her. "Tricia, I'd like you to meet Natalie Goode. She's one of our most popular campers. And you two have something in common. You both have famous fathers. Natalie's dad is Tad Maxwell. The movie star."

Natalie felt her heart sink. *One of the most popular campers? Her dad is a movie star?* She must sound like a total loser to Tricia! She was more popular than Natalie would ever be and her dad was *president*.

"Hey there," Tricia said with a friendly wave. "I've seen one of your dad's movies. It was pretty good."

"Thanks," Natalie stammered. All her worries about looking like a loser in front of Tricia disappeared. The whole "daughter of a famous actor" thing made Natalie think she could never be starstruck, but it turned out she was wrong! Natalie could see why Chelsea idolized Tricia so much. She'd only known her for less than a minute and she was already charmed by her sweet manner and cute style.

Dr. Steve noticed that Natalie was nervous, so he quickly jumped in. "Natalie is going to make sure you have a wonderful stay with us. She knows the camp inside and out, and she can help introduce you to the rest of the Walla Walla community."

"Wow, that's so nice of you, Natalie," replied Tricia. "Thanks."

"No problem at all," Natalie said with a grin. She was finally beginning to loosen up. "I think you're really going to like camp, Tricia."

"And who might you fellas be?" Dr. Steve glanced in the direction of the Secret Service guys and gave them a friendly smile.

The men's serious facial expressions did not

change one bit, but the tallest, skinniest one stepped forward and spoke.

"My name is Wharton." He pointed to the man on his left, who was shorter and rounder. "That's Jones." Then he pointed to the man on his right, who had a young face and freckles on his cheeks. "And that's Shepard."

"Well, ah, are you folks going to be, um, staying at camp?" Dr. Steve asked, clearly intimidated by Tricia's beefed-up bodyguards.

Natalie hoped that they wouldn't—they were kind of creeping her out at the moment.

"We're staying at a nearby motel and taking shifts so that Miss Tricia will be under constant surveillance. Is that acceptable?" Wharton asked.

Dr. Steve nodded. "Of course, that's fine. The camp has an extra car that you can use to travel back and forth."

A shrill bark from inside Tricia's pink animal carrier interrupted the conversation.

"I think Paris wants to be a security guard, too," Tricia cooed into her pink pet carrier. "Isn't that right, poochie?"

"Aw, she's so cute," Natalie said as she peered into the carrier's mesh window and spied Tricia's adorable dog panting away.

"Actually, she's barking because she's a bit claustrophobic," Tricia explained. "But she'll be fine as soon as I get her out of this thing."

"Umm . . . I'm sorry, Tricia, but we don't allow pets at camp," Dr. Steve said with a frown.

"Oh, no. Really?" Tricia's smile dropped.

Natalie couldn't stand the disappointment on Tricia's face. She didn't want anything to prevent her from having an amazing experience at camp. Suddenly a great idea popped into her head.

"Wait, Dr. Steve. What if we kept Paris in the nature hut? I'm sure she'd get along with the animals there. And that way Tricia can visit her whenever she wants."

Tricia's eyes lit up. "Paris is such a good dog. I promise she won't be any trouble."

"Sounds like the perfect solution," Dr. Steve said. "See? I knew you two would get along."

"Thanks so much," Tricia replied, and grinned at Natalie.

"Well, let's get going, then," Dr. Steve said, checking his watch. "Our hybrid is over in the parking garage. Follow me!"

When Dr. Steve walked ahead, Tricia whipped around and shook out her limbs as if she'd been cooped up like her dog. Then she began loudly chewing a piece of gum, which she must have been hiding under her tongue for their entire conversation.

"Hey, Nat," Tricia called out through a couple of chomps. "Could you, like, get me some snacks from the vending machine before we hit the road? My blood sugar is, like, totally bottoming out or something," Tricia added. "I'll have my peeps pay for it."

While Shepard began digging through his pockets for some change, Natalie did a double take. Was this the same well-spoken girl she'd been introduced to a couple minutes ago?

"Um, sure," Natalie said, completely stunned.

"She likes Skittles and Snickers," Shepard said before laying a few dollar bills in Natalie's hand.

"Thanks! You're the bestest!" Tricia shouted as she skipped off behind Dr. Steve, leaving Natalie in her dust.

"Natalie just called the front office from Dr. Steve's cell. They're only minutes away!" Chelsea shouted through two cupped hands.

Earlier that day, Chelsea and her bunkmates had decided to hold a surprise party for Tricia. It was the least they could do for the girl who had been described in last month's *Teen Vogue* as "an inspiring young member of American royalty."

At first, Chelsea had been in charge of cookie making, but after an hour of prep work, she had taken over the entire production. Chelsea wanted everything to be perfect for Tricia's arrival. Making a good impression was really important to her.

"How are the banners coming along?" Chelsea asked Priya and Brynn.

They held up a long piece of parchment paper with brightly colored letters that spelled out **WALLA WALLA ❤ TRICIA!**

It was obvious that Priya was proud of her work by the size of the grin on her face. "I think it's awesome."

Chelsea looked on with approval. "I just love

the glitter. That really makes a statement."

"It was such a smart idea. Thanks, Chelse," Brynn said.

"That's what I'm here for," Chelsea replied. "What about the gift bag?"

Sarah and Joanna scurried over to Chelsea holding a large wicker basket filled to the brim with goodies.

"There's a ton of cool stuff in here," Joanna said. "Like a Camp Walla Walla baby tee that's made out of hemp and some strawberry flavored Burt's Bees lip gloss."

"My mom sent me books off of my Amazon wish list, so I included a few beach reads she might like," added Sarah.

"Fantastic!" Chelsea was so pleased with how well everyone had worked together. She and her friends made such an amazing team. Tricia was sure to be blown away by this stellar greeting.

"Last item on the agenda is treats," Chelsea said with anticipation. She had skipped breakfast in order to get ready for the party, so she was pretty hungry.

Sloan and Jenna each held out a tray stacked high with delectable baked goods. The aroma of cookies and brownies wafted through the tent, making the air smell sweet.

"Jasmine supervised us in the kitchen," Sloan explained. "And everything is made completely with organic ingredients. I did the double chocolate chip cookies and the Rice Krispies treats."

Chelsea took a sample tasting of each, savoring

every delicious morsel on her tongue. "Wow, you really outdid yourself, Sloan!"

"Thanks," she replied.

Chelsea took a close look at what was on Jenna's baking pan and wrinkled her nose in dismay. "What's this supposed to be?"

"Banana nut bread," Jenna said with a sigh. "I kind of burned it. Sorry."

"How did that happen?" Chelsea asked, slightly irritated. Jenna was notorious for goofing off at all the wrong times.

"Does it matter? I can't UN-burn the bread," Jenna snapped.

"Wait—isn't Tricia's favorite food red grapes?" Sloan asked.

Chelsea's eyes lit up. She should have remembered that herself, given how psyched she'd been about Tricia coming to camp. But she'd totally forgotten. "Yes, you're right! Could you run over to the dining hall and see if they have any?"

"Actually, I know the girls in the next bunk have a stash of them. Be right back," Sloan said as she dashed out the door.

"Okay, everybody. Let's get into our positions. Tricia will be here any minute now," Chelsea instructed.

"Actually, the car just pulled up!" Joanna exclaimed as she peered out the window.

All the girls started giggling with excitement. "Okay, everyone grab hold of the banner," Brynn said.

Chelsea held her breath with anticipation. Any

second now, she'd be face-to-face with her idol!

"Hold on, are we saying 'Surprise, Tricia' or 'Welcome to Walla Walla'?" Sarah asked.

Before Chelsea could answer, the door of the tent flew open. Some of the girls said, "Welcome to Walla Walla," and some of them said "Surprise, Tricia!" Luckily, the only person to witness the confusion was Sloan.

"Got the grapes!" she proclaimed.

Chelsea sighed in relief. Thank goodness Tricia hadn't seen them mess up. "Great! Now hurry up and get in line."

Sloan darted over to an empty space near Priya and smiled.

Chelsea cleared her throat. "Okay, we're saying 'Welcome to Walla Walla.' Everybody got that?"

All the girls nodded.

The door creaked open again and in came Dr. Steve and Natalie, followed by Tricia and her adorable dog, Paris, who was being pulled along on a hot pink leash. There was also a stocky man with sunglasses next to Tricia who was checking out the place like he wanted to make sure it was safe.

"Welcome to Walla Walla!" the girls shouted as they proudly held up their homemade banner.

Chelsea's heart somersaulted when she saw the happy expression on Tricia's face.

"This is unbelievable," Tricia said with enthusiasm. "Thank you so much!"

"I'm going to let you girls get acquainted," Dr. Steve said as he placed Tricia's suitcases on the floor.

"Have fun! And don't forget to drop Paris off at the nature hut once you get settled."

"Oh, I will," Tricia said with a wink.

Chelsea couldn't stop staring at Tricia's eyelashes, which were lush and thick and perfectly curled. She thought about asking Tricia what kind of mascara she used, but when Chelsea thought about how sophisticated and important Tricia was, she figured her question would sound rather silly. In fact, she wasn't sure she should say anything now that she could finally have some one-on-one time with Tricia. She was so nervous, she was in distinct danger of stumbling over her words or doing something even more embarrassing.

"See you all at dinner tonight," Dr. Steve said and walked out the door.

Tricia's Secret Service man just stood there stiffly, with a stoic expression plastered on his face.

"Phew, I'm glad he's gone," Tricia said as she rolled her neck back and forth. Then she started chewing a piece of gum that seemed to magically appear in her mouth. "Now I can keep it real, ya know?"

Chelsea glanced around at the other girls. They looked just as baffled as she felt. Had Tricia's voice changed from prim-and-proper to tart-and-tangy, or had Chelsea just imagined it?

"Um, hello, sir," Priya said, presumably to the security guard. "Are you staying with us, too?"

Tricia laughed. "There is, like, no way I would let Jones cramp our style. He's just going to stand outside and follow me around a lot. And when he's not here, there's two others just like him to take his place. You just have to pretend like they're not around at all. Sound kosher?"

All the girls nodded their heads.

"Well, we have some things for you, Tricia. Just our little way of saying welcome to Walla Walla," Sloan said while the rest of the girls presented Tricia with the overstuffed gift basket and trays of goodies.

"You chicas are totally righteous!" Tricia yelped as she tore through the items like a toddler on Christmas morning. When she was done examining everything, she put the gifts to the side, flopped down on Sloan's bed, and put Paris on her lap.

"I bet you're tired from your trip to Vienna, aren't you?" Jenna asked.

Tricia mindlessly combed Paris's fur with her fingers. "My trip to where?"

"Vienna. You were there with your parents, right?" Natalie prompted.

"Oh, that was just a cover story," Tricia said matter-of-factly.

"Cover story?" Natalie asked with curiosity.

Chelsea couldn't believe it. Tricia was getting cooler by the nanosecond!

"Yeah, the administration's publicity people like to keep my image a certain way. It's just part of politics, that's all," Tricia explained.

"So where were you really?" Sarah inquired.

"Actually, I was in L.A. with Rob Pattinson."

The girls erupted in a frenzy of *oohs* and *aahs*.

"Don't tell anybody, but that boy likes

shopping more than *I* do!"

Everyone laughed and giggled at Tricia's joke, especially Chelsea. She was excited that Tricia's "real" personality seemed similar to her own. She had a feeling they were a lot alike!

"Wait a minute. Are you saying that all the stuff we found out about you on the Internet isn't really true?" Natalie asked, crossing her arms.

Chelsea threw Natalie a sharp look. Why was her friend all up in Tricia's face suddenly? Did it matter what anyone said about Tricia on the Web? She was here now, being honest with everyone, and that was the most important thing.

"I don't know, I stopped Googling myself a long time ago," Tricia said with a shrug. "But I do have to act a certain way in public. It's a drag, but whatever, I deal."

Chelsea grinned at Tricia. She absolutely loved this girl's attitude!

"Tell us more about L.A.," Chelsea blurted out. "Did you shop with anyone else famous?"

"Actually, guys, I'm supposed to take Tricia for a tour of the grounds now," Natalie interrupted. "Can this wait until later?"

Chelsea's cheeks flushed pink. She had spent all this time and energy preparing something special for Tricia's arrival. Why was Natalie trying to spoil it, especially when she knew how much meeting Tricia meant to Chelsea? Plus, Dr. Steve *had* said that he was leaving so all the girls could get to know one another better.

Then it occurred to Chelsea that Natalie was used to getting all the attention, what with being the daughter of a movie star and all. Could it be that Natalie was jealous of Tricia?

"Yeah, Nat and I made plans on the way over here," Tricia said as she hopped off the bed and put an arm around Natalie. "She's my special, personal guide while I'm here."

Chelsea's eyes widened to the size of volley-balls. *Special, personal guide?!*

"It was Dr. Steve's idea," Natalie added.

Chelsea swallowed hard. If she had written her own essay, maybe she'd be in Natalie's shoes right now. Life was so unfair.

"Later, ladies!" Tricia said as she tugged Paris behind her and followed Natalie out the door. Once Jones quickstepped behind the girls and out of the bunk, Chelsea took a moment to consider the glittery welcome sign her friends had made with disappointment. With Natalie stuck to Tricia like glue this week, Chelsea doubted that Tricia would get to know her at all, let alone become her best friend.

chapter SIX

"These are the best pancakes in the whole world," Jordan mumbled, his mouth full of pancakes. "Who'dda thunk going green would do such good things for the food around here?"

"You mean the whole *universe*," corrected Priya. The pancakes in question were buckwheat and made from scratch early that morning by Dr. Steve and some of the older campers.

"I don't know how you guys can even eat," David said through a long yawn. "I am so tired I can barely chew."

"Me too," said a weary-eyed Jenna. "Why does being green have to be such a sacrifice?"

"Come on, if the pioneers had to do this stuff, so can we," Sloan said as she licked some syrup off her fingers. "In fact, maybe we should have a pioneers skit for the festival or something."

"That's a cool idea," Jenna replied. "You should mention that at the meeting this afternoon." Jenna was talking about a Green Festival planning meeting scheduled for a little later in the day.

"Great, I will." Sloan's face lit up with excitement. She was glad that her friends were getting in the spirit, and hoped the meeting would be packed. In fact, she had made up some flyers (on 100 percent recycled paper) that she was going to post around camp to get buzz going so more people would show up for the meeting.

"So where are Natalie and Tricia?" Joanna asked, glancing around the dining hall. "I haven't seen them at all this morning."

Chelsea rolled her eyes. "They went on some lame early morning hike."

"Hike? But doesn't Nat *hate* hiking?" Connor asked.

"I know. Isn't she being kind of fake?" Chelsea replied.

Sloan rolled her eyes. Chelsea was definitely overreacting. Natalie was just doing what Dr. Steve had asked and giving Tricia some special attention.

"Nat isn't being fake, Chelse. Tricia probably asked her to go hiking and she was just being a good sport, that's all."

"Whatever," Chelsea huffed.

"I really loved hearing Tricia's stories over dinner last night," Sarah said, smiling. "I still can't believe that she flew on Air Force One with Ashley Tisdale!"

"Or had the Jonas Brothers play at her birthday party," added Priya.

"It's just weird that she's so different than we'd thought," Sarah said as she helped herself to a second glass of freshly squeezed orange juice.

Sloan nodded in agreement. They'd all found out over dinner that none of the Internet stuff Sloan had discovered was true. Not even the red seedless grapes part! Still, Tricia was a fun and vivacious girl who seemed more than happy to help use her celebrity for a good cause like Walla Walla's Green Festival. Did anything else really matter?

"It's a shame that she's only going to be here for one week," Chelsea said. "I doubt any of us will get a chance to know her all that well."

Sloan could see Chelsea's point. Tricia was only here for a few days and Chelsea seemed interested in spending time with Tricia—was there a way Sloan could help out somehow?

Hmmm . . . this might do the trick, she thought.

"You know what, Chelse? The committee is probably going to work with Tricia a lot in preparation for the festival."

"Yeah, so?" Chelsea huffed.

"Well, why don't you cochair the group with me? I'll need your help in prepping Tricia for her big speech on Sunday," Sloan suggested. "What do you think?"

"I think . . . you're *totally righteous!*" Chelsea shrieked, throwing her arms around her friend.

"So I guess this means you're in?" Sloan said, laughing.

"Of course!" Chelsea shrieked.

"Good, maybe now we won't have to listen to Chelsea's whining anymore," David joked.

"I don't whine. I'm just . . . intense, is all," Chelsea said with a grin.

Sloan chuckled under her breath—*overly dramatic* was more like it. Even so, Sloan was glad she'd asked Chelsea to be her partner. Together, they were going to make the Green Festival a weekend no one would ever forget!

▲ ▲ ▲

Before the first activities of the day began, Sloan had special permission to post her green flyers on the bulletin boards located around camp. A couple of times, campers came up to her while she was pinning up the flyers and told her they were going to come. She couldn't have been more pleased.

Until a certain someone surprised her while she was posting a flyer outside the boys' bunk.

"Hello again," a voice called from behind her.

Sloan turned around quickly and nearly dropped the remainder of her flyers when she saw Miles standing a few feet away. He was wearing a Camp Walla Walla baseball hat, which hid his friendly eyes a little bit and made it easier for Sloan to look at him. She was still embarrassed about the way she'd reacted to his comment on her essay—and even more embarrassed about the fact that he'd wound up being right. "Hey," she said sheepishly.

"I'm glad I caught you. I want to talk to you about the other day." Miles rubbed the back of his neck nervously. "I'm sorry for being a jerk."

Sloan gave him a little smile, feeling more at ease. It was cute that he wanted to apologize. "It's okay. You were just being honest with me. I shouldn't have gotten so upset. In fact, maybe if I'd listened to you I would have won the contest." Just then, Sloan realized that Miles had been looking out for her. Which was the nicest thing anyone could do for someone else.

Miles flashed Sloan a wide smile. "Well, I'm still sorry I hurt you, especially before I got the chance to really know you. Though my grandmother *does* say honesty is the best policy."

"So does mine," Sloan said with a giggle.

As Miles approached her, Sloan couldn't help but notice that he had the sweetest twinkle in his eyes. But he was also a little bit awkward, which Sloan found really charming.

"What's that?" Miles reached out for the flyers in Sloan's hand, and accidentally brushed up against her wrist. It sent little shivers up her arm.

Sloan giggled again and then froze for a second. *Ugh! Stop acting like such a ditz!*

"It's a flyer reminding everyone about tonight's Green Festival planning meeting."

Sloan felt her skin turn warm and tingly as she handed one to him.

"Nice," Miles said, quickly reading it over. "It's really cool that you're still so into this."

"Thanks," Sloan said, blushing. "Actually, Dr. Steve made me the committee chairperson yesterday, so I'm *really* involved."

"But I thought Natalie won the contest," Miles said, confused.

"She did, but she wound up being reassigned," Sloan said. "Isn't that great?"

"I guess," Miles said, adjusting his hat. "Was Nat mad or anything?"

"Nat seemed cool with it," she replied.

Miles shrugged. "I was just wondering. She seemed really excited when she won."

Sloan remembered the moment when Natalie's name was announced. At the time all she could think about was how bad it felt to lose. Now did she need to feel guilty about luck being on her side?

"Well, now she's the personal guide to the president's daughter. That's a pretty sweet trade if you ask me," Sloan said.

"If you like that kind of thing," Miles said. "Personally, I think the festival is more interesting."

Sloan grinned. "You do?"

"Yeah. My dad used to take me to the Bald Eagle Festival in Alaska every year. I loved it," Miles explained.

Sloan's heart fluttered a little bit. "Wow, that sounds amazing."

"So can I keep this flyer? I'd like to show it to some of my friends." Miles motioned to a group of boys hacky-sacking near one of the bunks.

Sloan grinned. She was happy that Miles was going to be in close proximity now that the two of them were on better terms.

"Sure, the more people we have helping out, the better," she replied.

"Great," Miles said. "See ya later at the meeting."

"See ya," Sloan said as she watched Miles wander off to his circle of friends, waving her flyer above his head.

chapter
SEVEN

When rest period finally rolled around, Natalie collapsed onto her bed. She was completely exhausted from her hike with Tricia, Cybil the nature counselor, and Wharton, the most athletic Secret Service agent in Tricia's security detail. Tricia had convinced both Natalie and Cybil that the hike was going to be a short little jaunt to jumpstart their morning, but they'd wound up covering almost all the trails around Camp Walla Walla, thanks to Tricia's unlimited supply of energy. Apparently Tricia was training for some type of marathon personally recommended by her friend Vanessa Hudgens. Marathons *definitely* weren't Natalie's thing.

As Natalie rubbed one of her aching calves, she tried to remind herself that looking after the president's daughter was a super-important task that she had been handpicked to do. Still, Natalie couldn't get rid of the heavy feeling inside her chest that told her choosing Tricia over a college app–building activity may have been a mistake. Tricia had been running Natalie ragged since she'd arrived and didn't seem to care one bit.

Then again, maybe I just hate hiking more than I thought I did, she thought.

Natalie closed her eyes for a brief moment, hoping that she could meditate her way into a good mood, but soon she was startled by a high-pitched scream. She leaped up and found Tricia standing on top of her own bed, frantic with fear.

"What's wrong?" Natalie asked worriedly.

"A bug!!!" squealed Tricia. She pointed at the floor, her hands shaking. "It's disgusting!"

Natalie glanced down at the bottom of Tricia's bed and saw a pretty sizable insect crawling around. What was even more disgusting was the mess that the insect was crawling around in. Natalie had no idea how Tricia had built a pile of candy bar wrappers and crumb-filled bags of cookies in less than twenty-four hours, but nevertheless, there it was. And if Natalie didn't act fast, more bugs would be on the way.

"Hold on, let me get something to capture it with," Natalie said.

"Oh, thank you, thank you, thank you," Tricia said in relief. "Bugs freak me out so bad!"

Natalie shook her head and laughed to herself. Sure, there may have been a time when she was prone to flipping out over little things like bugs, but honestly, wasn't Tricia too old to be acting like a frightened— and maybe a teensy bit spoiled—little girl?

Natalie used her reusable water bottle to scoop up the insect and then set it free a few feet outside the tent. When she returned to the bunk, she passed Wharton and Jones, who were in the middle of changing shifts. As Wharton walked off and Jones took his spot in front of the bunk, Natalie noticed that Jones had a huge, grease-stained bag from McDonald's in his hand.

There's a Mickey D's around here?!

"Excuse me, miss," Jones called out to her in a gravelly voice.

"Yes, sir?" Natalie responded.

"Would you mind bringing this to Tricia?" he asked.

Natalie was amazed. Tricia's bodyguards were expected to fetch her lunch, too? Incredible.

"Sure," she replied and took the bag of food.

As soon as Natalie opened the door, Tricia sprinted over and snatched the McDonald's bag from her.

"It's about time! I'm starving," Tricia squealed, digging into the bag. She pulled out a handful of french fries and popped them in her mouth. "You want some?" Tricia asked with her mouth full.

Natalie shook her head. "No, that's okay."

"Are you sure? There's plenty." Tricia sat on her bed and dangled the bag in front of her as though she were mistaking Natalie for her precious Cavadoodle.

"Really, I'm fine."

"Well, I can send Wharton or Shepard back out if you change your mind," Tricia said.

Natalie cringed a little. It seemed like Tricia expected everyone to accommodate her, regardless of if it inconvenienced them.

"Yes, he remembered!" Tricia exclaimed as she pulled a cardboard container out of the bag. Once Tricia pried the lid open, the smell of Big Mac wafted through the tent. "I like my burgers piping hot," she started. "And my iced tea super cold." And then, much to Natalie's disbelief, Tricia pulled out a large cup of iced tea. A large *Styrofoam* cup! How could Tricia, the Princess of Green, drink from a *Styrofoam* cup? Didn't she know that Styrofoam containers helped cause the deterioration of the ozone layer? Everyone else in the world did, including Tricia's dad, who was *president!* Maybe now was a good time for Natalie to educate Tricia a little bit. Perhaps then she would stop being so careless with her trash and become a little bit more eco-conscious.

"Listen, Tricia. Don't take this the wrong way, but—"

Natalie was interrupted by a pop rock song in the form of a ringtone echoing throughout the tent.

"One sec, Nat. That's my BF!" Tricia put her hamburger back in its container and reached for her phone.

"Wait—you're allowed to have a cell phone here?" Natalie asked.

"Yeah, my father called Dr. Steve and he said it was okay to bend the rules for me," Tricia said, smiling.

Natalie wasn't surprised. Who in their right mind would say no to the president?

"Hey, Puppy!" Tricia cooed into the phone. "Can I holler back at ya later? I've got the munchies.

Okay. Toodles!"

Once Tricia hung up, she grabbed her burger, pulled it out of its container, and took a giant bite. "Sorry, my boyfriend is, like, a ministalker. He just hates it when I'm away and calls every hour. Ugh. Like there's not enough drama in my life! I can't ever just relax and be me, ya know? But so far, I've been able to do that here, which is awesome."

Natalie sighed. Giving Tricia a lecture on being tidy and more environmentally aware seemed like a lame thing to do now, especially since she understood the sentiments behind Tricia's words. Natalie knew what it was like to be on display in a world where all eyes were on you. It was a lot of pressure, and not too many people could empathize like Natalie could. Maybe Tricia's sloppiness was just her way of kicking back and dealing with stress.

"Anyhow, what were you going to say?" Tricia asked through a mouthful of burger.

Natalie decided then and there to let things slide and cut Tricia some slack. It was the least she could do.

"Oh, I was going to hit up the supply room for some extra garbage bags and wanted to know if you needed anything."

"You are a *saint*," Tricia said. "Could you, like, pick up a package for me at Dr. Steve's office? I couldn't fit all my shoes into my suitcases, so I had them FedExed here."

"Uh . . . I guess—"

"And I ran out of Snickers bars. Could you hit

Jones up for a five spot and fetch a couple for me?"

"I suppose—"

"OH! And could you talk to someone about getting me private quarters? I really like staying with you girls, but as you can see, I need *lots* of room to spread out."

Wow, I am SO sorry I asked, Natalie thought.

"Fine, I'll see what I can do."

"Thanks, Nat!" Tricia said brightly. "I better call the boy back. He's probably checking my Facebook status this very minute, not like I can even update it here. One computer?! I don't know how you guys live like that."

Natalie waved good-bye and stumbled out into the warm summer air. It was a beautiful summer day, but Natalie couldn't even enjoy it. She had a job to do. For twenty minutes she searched high and low for anything resembling Snickers bars on the campgrounds. Aside from a semimelted Kit Kat that Natalie got from a CIT with a notorious sweet tooth, there were no chocolate bars of any kind to be found. Apparently Camp Walla Walla had traded all of them in for organic granola treats in biodegradable wrappers.

Luckily for Natalie, she *was* able to locate some more garbage bags, which Tricia needed way more than candy, even if she didn't know it. After stocking up on garbage bags, Natalie headed for Dr. Steve's office, where she would pick up Tricia's shoes (ugh) and speak with him about moving Tricia to a private bunk.

Natalie had no idea what to say to Dr. Steve.

What if he thought that Tricia wasn't enjoying her stay at Walla Walla and it was all Natalie's fault? Natalie considered telling Dr. Steve that Tricia was just very messy and wanted more room in which to make that mess, but then she felt like she was betraying her country or something.

Natalie figured she'd just make up some excuse on the fly when she got there. She really couldn't figure out a better way to explain the situation.

"Hey, Natalie," said Ben, one of the junior counselors at Walla Walla, who had an adorable smile, now that she thought about it.

"Hi there," Natalie replied. "I wanted to stop by and pick up a package for Tricia. Where can I find it?"

Ben laughed and gestured to the copy room on his left. "I think you're going to need some help. It's a pretty big box."

Natalie glanced over and saw a cardboard box the size of a forty-inch TV. "I'll take care of it later, then," she said, sighing in defeat. "Is Dr. Steve here? I have to ask him a question, and it's kind of important."

"No, he's at the Green Festival planning meeting," Ben said. "I'm surprised you're not there yourself."

Natalie's breath caught in her throat. *I can't believe I forgot about the meeting! ARGH!*

"Yeah, I was tied up most of today. Where is it again?" Natalie really hoped she could get to the meeting before it ended. Even if she wasn't chairperson, she still had a ton of ideas that she wanted to share!

"It's at the new rock garden. Sloan thought that

it was the perfect place to inspire everyone's imagination," Ben said.

Natalie felt the jealousy come on in waves. If she hadn't fallen for Dr. Steve's spiel about her being the perfect candidate to show Tricia around camp, she would be in charge of the committee instead of spending every waking moment being Tricia's errand girl! But she knew she had to shake herself free of those negative thoughts quickly—there was no time to lose!

"Thanks, Ben. I'll head over there," Natalie said.

Within seconds, Natalie was out of Dr. Steve's office and running as fast as she could across the campgrounds, the box of garbage bags in one hand and Tricia's Kit Kat in her back pocket. She managed to reach the rock garden in about three minutes flat. Unfortunately, by the time she got there, the meeting was already breaking up. Natalie watched in disappointment as Sloan shook hands with the counselors and fellow campers who had volunteered to help with the festival. She even saw a cute new boy camper standing next to Sloan with a huge grin on his face.

Natalie felt her heart sink, but when she saw Chelsea approaching, she put on a happy face.

"Hey, how did the meeting go?" Natalie asked, trying to seem chipper.

"It was really good. Can you believe this many people came?" Chelsea said enthusiastically.

Natalie bit her lip to keep herself from getting upset. "I know, Sloan did an amazing job of getting the word out."

"She sure did. So where have you been all day? I thought for sure you'd want to be here, after all that *work* you put into your essay," Chelsea said sarcastically.

Natalie's mouth dropped open in surprise at Chelsea's comment. She knew she hadn't been able to thank Chelsea properly yet for all her help with the essay, but did she really deserve that kind of snotty remark? It didn't make Natalie eager to express her gratitude, that was for sure.

"Oh, Tricia and I spent all morning hiking the trails with Cybil. Tricia's training to be in some marathon and—"

"Yeah, whatever." Chelsea looked over her shoulder intently, like she was hoping to find a way out of the conversation. "Anyway, I'd better get back to Sloan. We have so much organizing to do."

Natalie flinched. "*We?*"

"Oh, didn't you hear the news? Sloan and I are cochairing the committee together. Isn't that awesome?" Chelsea said with a fake smile.

Natalie's skin suddenly felt sunburn-hot. Why hadn't Sloan asked *her* to be cochair? Sloan knew how much it would have meant to her! Still, Natalie wanted to give Sloan the benefit of the doubt. Perhaps she had assumed Natalie would be too busy with Tricia to cochair the committee. Or maybe she had asked Dr. Steve if she could pick Natalie and he said no. Regardless of the reason, Natalie had to keep her emotions in check.

"Yeah, it is. Hope you have lots of fun," Natalie

said through slightly clenched teeth.

Chelsea gave Natalie a self-satisfied smirk. "Oh, I will."

When Chelsea spun around, Natalie squeezed the box of garbage bags so hard, it nearly crumpled.

chapter
EIGHT

Chelsea was not a big fan of Ultimate Frisbee, but like it or not, the game was on the morning exercise roster for all campers. So she dragged herself to the main activities field with the rest of her bunkmates, except for Natalie and Tricia. It was the second time in two days that the pair had been gone before anyone had the chance to wipe the sleep out of their eyes, and it was really getting on Chelsea's nerves, especially since Natalie knew how much Chelsea admired Tricia. Couldn't Natalie at least have asked her to tag along this morning?

Then again, Chelsea had been kind of nasty to Natalie yesterday, so it shouldn't have surprised her one bit. In fact, when Chelsea thought about the snarky attitude she took with her friend, it made her feel kind of nauseated. Natalie hadn't done anything wrong, so Chelsea really had no right to snap at her. Right now, she was feeling pretty terrible about it.

"Heads up!" a voice shouted from not so far away.

Chelsea snapped herself out of her thoughts just in time to spot a bright orange Frisbee flying her way. But it was too late—Chelsea couldn't duck out of the way in time, and it smacked her right in the face.

"OW!!!" she shrieked dramatically, rubbing the bridge of her nose. But before she had time to curse the moron who invented the Frisbee, she was surrounded by a group of counselors and campers ready to offer their assistance.

Jenna was the first to the scene. "Are you okay, Chelse?"

"No! That really hurt," Chelsea whimpered.

"I'm so so so so so sorry!" exclaimed Priya. "It was all my fault."

"You bet it was," countered Jordan. "Chelsea isn't even on your team. Why did you throw it at her?"

"I wasn't trying to! I was aiming for Joanna," Priya said.

David let out a chuckle. "Joanna was on the sidelines, Priya. She rotated out of the game after the last play."

"All right, enough, kids," Ellie interrupted. "Chelsea, are you hurt badly?"

"I'm seeing spots," Chelsea moaned. "And maybe even stripes."

"Do you want me to take you to the infirmary?" Ellie offered.

"I suppose," Chelsea muttered. *Anything is better than this stupid game.*

"Oh, please let me take her. I feel so awful," Priya interjected.

Chelsea sighed. This day was off to a terrible start.

"Okay, go ahead," Ellie said. "Everyone else, back to your positions. Sarah's team will have a time-out."

"Feel better, Chelse!" Brynn said as Priya walked Chelsea off the field.

"We'll score one just for you!" shouted Connor.

Chelsea gave her friends a limp wave, then wobbled alongside Priya to the infirmary.

Chelsea's visit to the infirmary was a short one, and thankfully, the extent of her injuries was a barely noticeable pink mark on the lower part of her nose. No permanent damage done. Afterward, Priya walked her back to their bunk so she could lie down.

"Are you sure you don't want me to stay with you?" Priya asked as she and Chelsea approached the tent's front door.

"It's okay, go finish the game," Chelsea said.

Priya smiled. "I will. Thanks for not being mad."

"You know what they say, 'don't get mad, get even,'" Chelsea said with a smirk.

Priya's smile dropped.

"I'm kidding, Priya. Geez, relax!"

Priya exhaled. "Phew! You nearly gave me a heart attack."

"See ya later," Chelsea said.

"See ya," Priya replied and dashed off down the path to the activities field.

Chelsea was happy to be at her bunk. She looked forward to having the place all to herself, but— surprise!—Tricia was there, listening to her iPod and dancing around the tent. *Score! Finally some alone time with*

Tricia, Chelsea thought, suddenly wishing she didn't have a big bandage on her nose.

Tricia stopped dancing as soon as she saw Chelsea staring at her, but she didn't seem embarrassed at all.

"Hey, Chelsea! How are you?" Tricia said loudly as she continued to bop to the music that was filtering through her earbuds.

It was enough to make Chelsea totally forget all about the morning and her near brush with death. "Great! Who are you listening to?"

"Katy Perry. She is *such* a sweetheart," Tricia said with a smile.

"You've met her?" Chelsea just couldn't believe how awesome Tricia's life was. Her stories were even more impressive than Natalie's.

"A bunch of times." Tricia turned off her iPod and threw it on her bed. "I love her fashion sense."

Chelsea grinned from ear to ear. "Me too! Did you see what she was wearing at the MTV Video Music Awards?"

"Only Katy can pull off zebra print hot pants," Tricia replied.

"She got them at H&M y'know . . ." Chelsea trailed off.

"No way!" Tricia's eyes twinkled. "Wow—you're even more plugged in than I am—and I *know* the girl. Can we just follow each other around 24/7?"

Chelsea's head almost exploded. Tricia thought she was plugged in? *This must be what heaven is like!*

Just as Chelsea was going to say something

witty in reply, Natalie stormed into the room, looking rather disheveled and tired. It was obvious by the scowl on her face that she was in a bad mood.

"Okay, Tricia. I loaded the last piece of your luggage and packages on the golf cart. Are you ready to go?" Natalie said as she redid her ponytail and wiped the sweat off her brow.

"Almost. Chelsea and I were just chatting," Tricia chirped.

"Go? Where are you going?" Chelsea asked.

She hoped that Tricia wasn't leaving Camp Walla Walla early. Just when they were starting to bond!

"Oh, Natalie got us a sweet hookup. She and I are moving into one of the vacant counselors' bunks," Tricia explained.

Chelsea crossed her arms in front of her chest and stared at Natalie. "Is that so?"

"Don't look at me, it wasn't my idea," Natalie said curtly.

Tricia walked over to Natalie and threw an arm around her. "She's right—I'm to blame! I'm just used to having a bigger room is all. And I couldn't get along without Natalie. She's the bestest!"

Chelsea felt a hot wave of jealousy wash over her, but when she saw Natalie roll her eyes at Tricia, it infuriated her even more. If Natalie didn't want to be Tricia's sidekick, then why didn't she let Chelsea do it?

"Just let me run to the bathroom and we'll be on our way," Tricia said to Natalie. "Back in a sec."

Chelsea squared off against Natalie once Tricia

left the bunk and gave her a stern look.

"What's wrong?" Natalie asked, clearly frustrated.

"Nothing. You just seem tired, like you can't keep up with Tricia," Chelsea said matter-of-factly. She knew this type of snippy comment might aggravate Natalie, but Chelsea couldn't hold back.

"She's a lot to handle." Natalie sat down on her bed and rolled her neck back and forth. "I doubt the president can keep up with her, either."

"Well, maybe you just need to be more energetic," Chelsea replied. "You know, like me."

Natalie glanced at Chelsea and chuckled. "Could you be any more obvious?"

"What do you mean?"

"If you want to room with Tricia, just say so," Natalie said.

Chelsea hadn't thought of that, but it was a great idea. She couldn't contain her excitement. "That would be awesome!"

"Fine with me. I could use a break," Natalie said, rubbing her feet.

"Thanks so much, Nat!" Chelsea said.

All of a sudden, Tricia burst through the door. "I'm back!" she sang.

Chelsea smiled widely. This was so surreal! She had always wanted to meet Tricia in person, and now she was going to share a bunk with her. How amazing was that?

"Hey, Tricia, can I make a suggestion?" Natalie asked.

"Sure. What's up?" she replied.

Chelsea was already starting to think about the fun things she and Tricia were going to do. Manicures and pore shrinking face masks and gossiping and sharing clothes . . . Chelsea could imagine the possibilities.

"Maybe it would be better if Chelsea roomed with you instead," Natalie finished.

Tricia looked confused. "But . . . you're my personal guide."

The bewildered expression on Tricia's face worried Chelsea. Maybe this wasn't such a good idea after all.

"Chelsea's much better than a personal guide. She's your biggest fan! No, she's more than a fan—she's *the* source for Tricia gossip! What could be better than that?!" Natalie said with all the enthusiasm she could muster.

Chelsea wanted to grab her pillow and throw it at Natalie's head. She wasn't supposed to tell *anyone* that, especially not *Tricia*!

Tricia glanced at Chelsea and stared at her awkwardly. "You are?"

Chelsea had no clue how to respond. If she said, "Of course not," then she'd sound kind of mean, but if she said "Yes, I am," didn't that make her sort of a stalker? This was probably the most awkward moment of her life.

"Yeah, she actually has the same shirt you wore on Oprah," Natalie added.

On the other hand, maybe *this* was the most

awkward moment of her life.

"That's . . . great," Tricia said, a little unnerved.

Natalie turned to Chelsea and winked at her, as if to say, "Who's your daddy?"

But Chelsea just glowered back at her. If Natalie thought she was helping matters, she was certainly wrong, wrong, WRONG! After learning that piece of private information, Tricia probably thought Chelsea was a gigantic loser.

"So what do you say, Tricia?" Natalie asked. "Want to trade campers?"

Chelsea wasn't about to let Tricia answer—she was way too humiliated to bunk with Tricia now.

"That's okay, Nat. You two should stick together," Chelsea said quickly, trying not to let on that she was embarrassed and upset.

Natalie frowned. "Are you sure?"

"Yes, I'm sure," Chelsea replied.

Tricia was visibly dying to make a break for it. "Well, we should be off then. Our tricked-out pad awaits!" she said, turning on her heels. She smiled at Chelsea, then waved good-bye. "Toodles!"

Tricia linked arms with Natalie, who was practically dragging her feet.

Chelsea grabbed a pillow and put it over her head so Jones the bodyguard wouldn't hear her cry.

NINE

On Tuesday afternoon, Sloan and the rest of the campers dressed in their swimsuits and gathered at the lake for a canoeing activity. While all of her bunkmates chattered with each other, Sloan trained her eyes on her notebook. Tonight was the second Green Festival meeting and she wanted to be prepared.

Sloan was super-psyched about how the planning was going—the group had already started making flyers to put up in town and picked out a delicious array of food for the menu. All they needed to do was decide what kind of entertainment they should have, as well as what Tricia should talk about during her speech. That was going to be the highlight of the festival for sure!

"Okay, everyone, listen up," Jasmine said in a loud, upbeat voice.

Sloan closed her notebook, put it in her canvas knapsack, and gave Jasmine her full attention.

"We're going to start breaking up into teams of four. Three campers and one counselor," Jasmine continued. "And then we're going to have a little race from the east dock to the west dock."

Some of the kids in the crowd threw their arms up in the air and said, "Sweet!" while some others whined, "Do we have to?"

Jasmine just smiled. "All right, everyone grab a life vest, and once you've done that, pick your team and then meet up with a counselor near a canoe."

"Yes! This is going to be great!" Jenna said.

"I'm on your team," Connor said to Jenna.

"What about me?" Brynn asked.

Sarah put her arm around Brynn. "There's room for you in my canoe."

"Nat's on my team," called a voice in the crowd.

Sloan saw Natalie helping Tricia on with her life jacket. The frown on her friend's face was the size of a jumbo hot dog.

"Gimme a break," another voice muttered.

Sloan peered over her shoulder and saw Chelsea grimacing as she strapped on her own life jacket. She looked as though she'd swallowed an entire grapefruit. *Geez, why is everyone in such a bad mood?*

As far as she was concerned, life was pretty good these days. She was enjoying camp so much, and it was only going to get better as the Green Festival approached.

Sloan was brought back to reality by a tap on her shoulder.

"Do you have a spot on your team for me?"

Sloan spun around and saw Miles standing beside her. His hair was a little messy from the light wind outside and he was flashing his adorable, toothy grin.

"Of course I do," Sloan said, her voice shaking a little.

"Great. I'm a really gifted rower," he joked.

"Wow, I can't wait to see it," Sloan said, smiling.

"Sloan, Miles, why don't you join me and Chelsea," Jasmine called out.

"Okay," Sloan replied dreamily. Jasmine could have asked her if she wanted to be on a team with Michael Phelps and she wouldn't have noticed. Sloan only had eyes for Miles.

As she and Miles wandered over to Jasmine and Chelsea, they were approached by Natalie and Tricia (and Tricia's bodyguard Shepard, who was wearing a life jacket over his navy suit).

"Hey, guys," Tricia said, ever so bubbly.

"Hi, Tricia," Sloan replied, finally turning away from Miles.

Chelsea managed a weak hello under her breath, while Natalie merely waved as if she were swatting at a fly. Sloan thought that both of the girls were acting a little weird, but didn't think now was the proper time to ask if anything was wrong.

Tricia put her arm around Natalie. "I just wanted to invite you all over to our new digs to hang out and chill," Tricia said. "Ellie agreed to chaperone and everything. Please come!"

"You and Nat have your own bunk? That's really cool," said Miles. "When is the party, exactly?"

"We were thinking about doing it after the

Green Festival meeting," Natalie mumbled. "I'm sure everyone will want to kick back and relax after a couple hours of planning."

"That's a great idea, Nat," Sloan said brightly, happy that her friend thought to plan around her meeting. "We'll be there." She made eye contact with Miles and they both smiled.

"Awesome! See you guys later," Tricia said, then traipsed off to Ellie's canoe with Natalie and Shepard.

Chelsea mumbled something again once they all walked away.

"What did you say, Chelse?" Sloan asked.

"I said I'm not going to the party." Chelsea stormed over to the dock, grabbed an oar, and hopped into the canoe.

"What's the matter with her?" Miles asked.

Sloan had a feeling that whatever was bothering Chelsea had something to do with Natalie. But she didn't want to burden Miles with the girls' silly drama, so she just answered, "No idea."

"Okay, people! The first match up will be Ellie's team versus my team," Jasmine yelled through cupped hands. "David, you can sound the horn once we're ready."

"Nice!" David replied, grabbing the air horn off the dock.

Sloan and Miles followed Chelsea over to the dock, picked up their oars, and got into the canoe. Jasmine grabbed an oar for herself and then sat at the front of the boat.

"Good luck, you guys!" Tricia shouted from

the other side of the dock. She was sitting in between her bodyguard and Natalie. Ellie was perched in front of the boat, just like Jasmine.

Sloan and Miles laughed in unison while Chelsea brooded in the back of the boat.

"Spoken like someone who has never been to camp before," Miles joked.

Once everyone was settled in their boats, Jasmine said, "Okay, David, whenever you're ready!"

David nodded. "On your mark, get set, GO!" he shouted, and then sounded the horn.

As soon as she uncovered her ears, Sloan started to paddle. Miles kept time with her perfectly—he didn't miss a beat. Sloan glanced over to Ellie's canoe and saw that her team was already lagging behind. Sloan gripped her oar and paddled some more, but soon she realized that Chelsea was making their canoe move as fast as a freight train. In fact, she was pumping her arms so quickly that Sloan worried they might pop out of their sockets.

"Way to go, Chelse!" Jasmine said as they continued to propel forward.

"We're getting closer!" Miles's oar tore through the water at a frantic pace, but he still wasn't as fast as Chelsea.

Sloan was trying to keep up, but was having a hard time.

"You can do it, Sloan! We're halfway there!" shouted Jasmine.

Sloan could feel her breath cutting through her throat. Her arm muscles were aching and they'd only been rowing for a few minutes. Sloan could hear Chelsea grunting each time she plunged her oar in the water, and her intensity unnerved her a little bit.

"We're neck and neck," Miles yelled over the sound of water splashing around them.

Sloan looked over at the other boat again. From the strained expression on Tricia's bodyguard's face, she could tell he was having the same difficulties that Sloan was.

"Go team, go!" Jasmine called out, willing her boat to reach the west dock first.

And that might have happened if Sloan's oar hadn't gotten caught on a large piece of log that no one saw until it was right in front of them. Sloan wasn't quick enough to let go of the oar and the bow of the boat shook hard. Jasmine slipped out of her seat and into the deep water a few feet away.

"Aaaahh!" she shrieked as she plunged into the cold lake.

"Omigod!" Sloan screamed. Even though Jasmine had her life jacket on, Sloan was scared that her counselor might be hurt.

"I'll get her," Miles said, not even hesitating before diving into the water after Jasmine.

Chelsea turned around to look at Sloan, her eyes tearing up. "I hope she's okay."

Sloan heard a second splash. Tricia's bodyguard had dived into the lake water as well and was swimming toward them. Seconds later, Miles resurfaced with his arm around Jasmine, who seemed stunned but fine. When Shepard reached them, he helped Miles get Jasmine back into the boat.

"I'm all right, girls, just very startled, that's all," Jasmine said, her teeth chattering.

Sloan breathed a big sigh of relief as Chelsea wiped at her eyes.

Ellie's boat had rowed over right away. Everyone in that canoe looked very concerned.

"Are you okay?" Natalie asked Jasmine.

"I'm fine, really," she replied.

As Miles and Shepard climbed back into their respective boats, Sloan could hear everyone from the east dock cheering and clapping.

"That was terrifying," Tricia said, sighing.

"To everyone except Miles," Sloan said.

She had to admit, she was really impressed with how brave he was, thinking on his feet and jumping in after Jasmine like that. Not everyone would be so calm and decisive under pressure.

"Boy Scout training comes in handy sometimes," Miles said as he wrung his shirt out.

"Let's turn around and get back to the dock," Ellie suggested.

Sloan's eyes locked with Miles's as the canoes started to drift apart on the water. Any awkward feeling she had toward him had completely faded away.

"So, how are you going to top that this summer?" Sloan asked him with a warm smile.

"I guess we'll have to wait and see," he replied with a wink, then turned his back to Sloan and began to row.

The second Green Festival meeting was underway on Tuesday afternoon and Sloan was all business, no play, even after that scare at the lake. The big weekend was only a few days from now, and although her team was off to a good start, Sloan knew that time was not on their side.

"Okay, everyone. Let's get started. We have a lot of work to do," Sloan said to the crowd of campers and CITs gathered at the rock garden.

Sarah raised her hand and waved it so that she could get Sloan's attention.

"What's up, Sarah?" Sloan asked.

"Do you think if we break up into groups we might get more done?"

Sloan smiled. "That's a great idea. If everyone could split up and focus on a particular part of the festival, we'd accomplish our goals a lot quicker."

Within a few minutes, everyone had assembled in groups, just like Sloan asked. Brynn, Joanna, and Sarah were in charge of putting together a skit for entertainment. Priya and Jenna were trying to assemble a small band of campers to sing a few old nature-themed folk songs from the 1960s.

The pack of boys at the meeting, which included David, Jordan, and Connor, all volunteered to be on the set-up crew. All the boys except for one, that is. Miles had offered to help Chelsea and Sloan shoulder the huge responsibility of handling the most important part of the festival—Tricia's keynote speech. Sloan was so happy he was interested in working closely with her. Maybe after all this planning was over they could—

"Are you ready yet?" Chelsea interrupted Sloan's train of thought. She was standing next to Miles with her hands on her hips, looking as sour as she had this afternoon.

"I know I am," Miles said, smiling.

Sloan grinned back at Miles, who was wearing a vintage T-shirt and yet another perfectly worn-in baseball cap. "I was born ready."

"So, where is Tricia, anyway? If we're going to be talking about her speech, shouldn't she be here?" Miles inquired.

"Good question. I have no idea where she is," Sloan replied.

"She's probably busy with Natalie, getting ready for her party," Chelsea said curtly.

"Well, I guess we can talk with Tricia while we're there," Sloan said.

"I told you already, I'm not going," Chelsea snapped.

Sloan flinched a bit at Chelsea's sharp tone. She knew that Chelsea was annoyed that Natalie was spending so much time with Tricia, but why wasn't she over it yet? There had to be something else that was putting Chelsea on edge. Perhaps she and Nat had gotten into a fight.

"Um, then why don't we throw around a few ideas now, narrow them down and then run a couple by Tricia tomorrow?" Miles suggested.

"That makes sense." Sloan was happy to have Miles around as a buffer. Aside from their strange first meeting, Sloan thought he was so easy to be around.

Chelsea was silent for a moment, thinking. Then her eyes lit up. "I know! She should talk about famous people."

Sloan sighed.

This is going to be the longest meeting ever.

"Like famous people and their charities?" Miles questioned.

"Well, I guess you could go that route," Chelsea said, annoyed. "I just think the audience might find it boring."

"I don't mean to be difficult here," Miles began, his cheeks turning a little pink. "But shouldn't Tricia speak on a topic that's more connected to the theme of the festival?"

"Okay, let's see what Sloan thinks," Chelsea said.

Miles shrugged. "Fine with me. What's your opinion, Sloan?"

Sloan's stomach began to churn with anxiety. She didn't want to play referee here, but that was part of being cochairperson. And while Chelsea was her friend, Sloan agreed with Miles. She had to stay true to her instincts, for the sake of the festival.

Sloan took a deep breath and spoke her mind. "I think Miles is right. Celebrity stories don't seem very relevant to the festival. Sorry, Chelsea."

"Suit yourselves," Chelsea said with a frown.

There was a long, tension-filled silence before Miles piped up with another idea.

"What if Tricia talked about what kids across the country are doing to protect the environment?"

Sloan practically pumped her fist in the air. "That's perfect!"

Miles grinned widely. "You really think so?"

"Yes, I do," Sloan said, her lips curling up into a soft smile.

"Are you guys forgetting that I'm cochair? I should get a say in this, too," Chelsea insisted.

Sloan and Miles's happy moment was instantly deflated by Chelsea's prickly attitude. Still, Chelsea was in the right. Sloan had asked her to cochair this committee, so she was entitled to have a strong voice in the matter.

"Of course," Sloan said, her voice strained. "What are your thoughts?"

As Chelsea cleared her throat, Sloan hoped that she wouldn't say anything harsh.

"Frankly, I think Tricia would rather talk about her *dog* than what Miles is suggesting," Chelsea said.

Forget harsh! That's harsh to the tenth power, Sloan thought.

Whatever was eating at Chelsea now had her lashing out at people she barely even knew. Sloan couldn't ignore it any longer.

"Hey, Miles, could you give me and Chelsea a second to talk privately?" Sloan hoped he'd be understanding.

"No problem," he said good-naturedly, and began to wander in the direction of a different group.

As soon as Miles was out of earshot, Sloan

began to question her friend.

"Chelse, it's obvious that you are upset about something. What is it?"

"Nothing. I'm fine," Chelsea said tersely.

"C'mon, you can tell me," Sloan reassured her. "And it'll stay just between us."

Chelsea buried her face in her hands for a moment and then looked up at Sloan sympathetically. "I'm sorry. I know I've been kind of moody today. And I feel awful about how I'm acting. I really do. It's just—"

Sloan waited for Chelsea to finish her sentence, but she got so choked up, she couldn't.

Once she took a big gulp of air, Chelsea said, "I'm going to take a short walk, okay? I'll see you back at the tent later."

Sloan's shoulders slumped forward. She was so disappointed that Chelsea wouldn't open up to her and allow her to help. "All right."

"And could you tell Miles that I'm sorry?" Chelsea added.

"Sure," Sloan replied.

"Thanks." Chelsea began to walk away, but she stopped for a moment and turned around to add, "Have fun at Tricia's party."

Sloan just smiled, then watched Chelsea slink through the rock garden as the sun began to set in the early evening sky.

chapter TEN

"Turn the music up, Nat! We need to get our groove on!" Tricia shouted as she mingled among a big cluster of adoring Walla Walla campers. Natalie grimaced, turning up the volume of the i-deck a notch. This was the twentieth order that Tricia had flung at her today, and she was getting kind of tired of obliging. True, Dr. Steve had asked her to stick by Tricia and make her feel at home, but being her gopher was above and beyond the call of duty, wasn't it?

"This is one sweet jam," Priya said, dancing alongside Brynn.

"Nat, you are so lucky! I'd give any- thing to stay here with Tricia," Sarah said. "She's ridiculously fun!"

"Yeah, I'm kind of jealous," Joanna added.

Natalie bit her lip to stop herself from telling her friends what hanging out with Tricia was really like. She wanted to be honest, but didn't have it in her to give Tricia a bad rep.

"I guess," was all Natalie could say.

"This sure beats planning the Green Festival,"

Jenna said. "I had no idea how much work it was going to be."

Natalie sighed with regret. She would die to switch places with Jenna. Natalie wasn't getting much out of her time spent with Tricia except the blisters on her feet from running around at Tricia's beck and call. If she hadn't given up the committee chairperson job, she'd probably be much happier.

"Well, I'm having a great time," said a chipper voice from behind Natalie.

Natalie and her friends turned around to see Sloan standing beside the cute new boy, Miles. They were both all smiles, like they'd discovered buried treasure or something.

"When did you guys get here?" Jordan asked.

"Just a minute ago. Sorry we're late. Sloan and I lost track of time at the rock garden," Miles replied with a small smile.

All the girls raised their eyebrows, including Natalie. It seemed as though their friend had a not-so-secret admirer.

"Anyway, Jasmine just walked us over here, and we're ready to party," Sloan said cheerfully.

"Awesome," said Jenna. "Tricia is such a blast. She's been cranking some great tunes."

"Is there anything to drink?" Miles asked.

"Yeah, Ellie brought over some organic fruit punch. It's delish," Priya said. "Want some?"

"Sure," Miles said, then turned to Sloan. "Should I get you a cup?"

Sloan blushed. "Yes, thanks."

Natalie felt a twinge in her chest. What she wouldn't give for a crush right now! At least then she'd have something to be psyched about. Sloan was so lucky—she had the perfect summer-camp job to add to her college app *and* a hot guy who obviously liked her.

Natalie felt a tug on her arm. It was Sloan, and she looked kind of worried.

"Hey, Nat, can I speak to you outside for a minute?" Sloan asked.

Natalie heard the concern in her friend's voice and knew whatever she had to say was important. "Okay."

She and Sloan walked outside to the front of the tent, where Tricia's bodyguard Wharton was standing at attention. Natalie felt a little weird about pretending like he wasn't there, but that's what Tricia had said to do, so she didn't acknowledge him at all.

"What's up?" Natalie was kind of hoping that Sloan needed some extra help with the Green Festival. That would definitely make her day.

"It's Chelsea," Sloan said.

Chelsea?

"What about her?"

Sloan glanced at Wharton, as if to make sure he wasn't eavesdropping, then continued. "She's seemed really bent out of shape these past couple of days. I was wondering if you knew anything about it."

Natalie was confused. "Of course I don't. Why?"

"Well, Chelsea seemed kind of annoyed at you

for spending so much time with Tricia and—"

"Wait a second," Natalie interrupted. She had a feeling that Sloan was about to say that Chelsea's funk was somehow her fault. That couldn't be further from the truth! "I tried to switch places with Chelsea so that she could room with Tricia and she totally backed out."

Sloan started at Natalie, clearly puzzled. "Oh, really?"

Natalie nodded.

"But why would she make a point of telling me she wasn't going to come to the party?" Sloan asked quizzically. "It was like she wanted to avoid you guys."

Natalie was starting to get annoyed. Sloan had all these things going for her this summer—including the job Natalie wanted. Did she have to play the role of chief busybody, too?

"Look, Sloan. Tricia and I invited Chelsea to come, just like everyone else. I don't know why she's so upset, or why you're being so nosy."

Natalie didn't like the curt tone of her own voice, but she couldn't control herself. She was just so tired of dealing with Tricia, and it was making her kind of short-tempered.

"I'm not being nosy. I'm just looking out for my friends," Sloan said firmly.

Natalie's cheeks burned red, and she could feel her pulse quicken. Was Sloan trying to insinuate that Natalie *didn't* look out for her friends? Because that would be way off base. All she'd been doing for the past two days was looking out for people—everyone except *herself*, in fact.

"Are you trying to say that I'm a bad friend or something?"

Sloan started to backpedal. "No, I'd never say anything like that."

Getting into an argument with Sloan wasn't going to do much good, and Natalie knew that if she said anything else, that would certainly happen.

"I'm going back inside, Sloan." Natalie spun around and walked toward the tent without looking back at her friend.

But before she could open the tent door, it slammed open. Tricia stood in the doorframe, all wide-eyed and happy-faced.

"There you are!" she exclaimed so loudly that Wharton winced a little bit. "I've been looking all over for you."

What I wouldn't give to be invisible, Natalie thought.

"We ran out of treats, so I talked Ellie into taking all of us to the dining hall for some post-party ice cream. Then we're all going to the nature hut to play with Paris. She hasn't been feeling well lately," Tricia explained, nearly tripping over her words with excitement. "Are you guys coming?"

Natalie peered over her shoulder at Sloan, who appeared to have all but forgotten about the tense conversation they'd just had.

"Sounds great," Sloan said. "Lead the way."

"What about you, Nat?" Tricia asked.

Natalie searched her feelings and realized that

she wasn't in the mood for ice cream or socializing. Some quiet time was what she needed, for sure.

"I think I'm going to sit this one out, Tricia," Natalie said. "You guys go ahead."

"Oh, okay," Tricia said, sounding disappointed. Then she turned around and shouted out the crowd behind her, "Hey, everyone! Let's get out of here, like, pronto!"

Natalie glanced behind Tricia and saw the entire group cheer, even Ellie, who at the moment seemed more like a camper than a counselor.

"See you later, roomie!" Tricia said, hugging Natalie tightly.

Oh brother, Natalie thought.

As the crowd filtered through the door, everyone said good-bye and thanked Natalie for her hospitality, one by one.

When Natalie entered the bunk, she was surprised by how clean it looked. There wasn't a stray piece of garbage to be found anywhere in the tent. Natalie smiled proudly. Maybe Tricia had turned over a new leaf.

Given that it was a hot summer night, Natalie thought she might take a quick three-minute shower. It would certainly be a nice way to relax. She went to the closet that she and Tricia shared in search of her pink terrycloth bathrobe. But when she opened the closet door, Natalie was showered with an avalanche of trash.

Once the last piece of garbage fell out of the closet, Natalie looked down at her feet. She couldn't believe the amount of debris! It was enough to attract a small bear or baby bobcat. She could tell from the pile of greasy McDonald's bags that this wasn't trash from the party. Tricia had created this disaster all by herself.

I guess this is Tricia's idea of pre-party cleaning. Ugh!

Natalie found the box of garbage bags that she'd picked up earlier and began to fill them with junk food wrappers and Styrofoam containers and plastic water bottles. She could feel her blood pressure rising with every item she tossed in the bags. Acting as Tricia's maid sure wasn't what Natalie had signed on for.

After Natalie cleared out the room and tied up the last of the bags, she spotted a folded-up note that must have fallen onto the floor while she was cleaning. On the front it read FOR NAT, and on the back, FROM TRICIA.

"More like Trash-a," Natalie mumbled to herself.

Natalie opened the note.

Thanks for a great party—you're such a good friend! Smooches, T

Natalie could not believe her eyes. *Good friend?* She felt more like a personal assistant to Tricia than a friend.

Maybe Tricia had led such a privileged life that she just couldn't tell the difference.

chapter ELEVEN

The last place Chelsea wanted to be on Wednesday morning was a nature walk. Everyone was all atwitter because Dr. Steve announced that the *National Gazette* was sending their reporters to the Green Festival. Chelsea didn't feel up to chatting with her friends about the *Gazette* or anything else for that matter. Who cared if some dumb newspaper was coming? Basically Chelsea was tired of all things green. All she wanted to do was hide out somewhere, but the nature walk was a mandatory activity—for everyone except Tricia and Natalie, of course. Apparently the nature counselor had excused them because Tricia wanted Natalie and Ellie—and Jones, of course—to take her horseback riding.

"Maybe if we collect enough wild berries on this walk we can serve them to the *National Gazette* people," Priya said as she plucked a handful of blueberries out of a tall bush and dropped them into a white bucket.

"With a side of homemade ice cream," Sarah added.

David licked his lips. "That sounds delicious."

Brynn knelt down and picked up some wild-flowers that were growing along a narrow part of the nature path. "Some of us could wear these in our hair, like this. That'll catch some attention."

She took a piece of the stem and tucked it behind her ear.

"Not me!" Jordan exclaimed, making everyone laugh.

"Count me out, too," Jenna said with a frown. "I'm a *classic* tomboy, which means dirt under my fingernails, not lavender in my hair."

"That's so gross," Joanna said.

"Can you talk some sense into Jenna, Chelse? She's going to ruin our chances of being spotted by the *Gazette* reporter," Priya pleaded.

Chelsea sat cross-legged on a large, smooth rock, braiding three blades of grass together. She was deep in thought and oblivious to what her friends were talking about. She kept replaying the moment Natalie told Tricia about that stupid shirt, and how Tricia had looked kind of creeped out by it. Each time she recalled how embarrassed she was, she got more irate. Chelsea had stood by her word and hadn't told anyone about Natalie's essay. Why couldn't Natalie have kept Chelsea's secret, too?

Suddenly a pair of fingers snapped in front of Chelsea's face and brought her back to reality.

"What? Did I miss something?" Chelsea asked.

Sloan was standing in front of her with an impatient look on her face. "How about our entire conversation?"

"Sorry, I was just—"

"Daydreaming?" Sloan interjected. "We could see that. What about?"

"Oh, nothing. I was just . . ." Chelsea nibbled on her lip, trying to come up with a good story. "Thinking about what I might say if I'm interviewed by the *Gazette*. I don't want to seem like a babbling idiot."

"Are you kidding? You could never seem like that," Sloan said with a friendly smile.

"Yeah, well, I think I'm going to sneak back to the tent and jot some things down on paper. I'd hate to lose this train of thought." Chelsea hoped her friends would buy this excuse and cover for her. She really wasn't in the mood to commune with nature.

"Okay, if anyone asks, you're sick or something," Sloan said as the rest of the girls nodded along.

"Thanks." Chelsea gave Sloan a quick hug and ducked behind a tree while the rest of the group wandered off behind the counselor, who was too busy pointing out types of foliage to notice Chelsea's departure.

Once they were out of sight, Chelsea tiptoed down the nature path, back the way she had come. She intended to stop by the resource center and nestle down with a good magazine—perhaps a fun "Is He into You?" quiz would help get her out of this funk. But when she walked by Tricia and Natalie's new living quarters, her feet suddenly came to a halt.

Even though Chelsea was angry at Natalie for embarrassing her, and felt too humiliated to hang out with Tricia, she regretted not going to the party last night. Everyone had been talking over breakfast about what a great time they had, and she felt like such an outsider. It was the worst feeling in the world.

If Natalie hadn't opened her mouth, none of this would be happening, she thought.

Chelsea was just about to walk away when she smelled something rotten that seemed like it was coming from the back of tent. Curious, she followed the scent behind the bunk, where she discovered a huge, slightly open garbage bag with flies hovering above it.

Ick, that's so nasty! she thought.

Chelsea pinched her nose with her fingers, leaned over, and took a better look. Inside, there were countless Styrofoam containers and plastic water bottles, and even some crushed, grease-soaked paper containers that had once held McDonald's french fries.

She was completely stunned. How could two girls generate so much trash, especially when one of them was the daughter of the supposedly "green" president of the United States? Then she saw a crumpled up piece of paper on the top that read NATALIE. It looked like a handwritten note.

Chelsea swallowed hard and gingerly picked the piece of paper out of the trash. When she opened it up and read it, her anger at Natalie began to grow. *Such a good friend . . . ? Puhleeze!* thought Chelsea. What kind of good friend couldn't keep a secret?

Chelsea dug into the pockets of her khaki shorts and pulled out her digital camera, which she'd brought along for the nature walk. She aimed her camera at the garbage bag and took a few pictures of it. Then she dashed over to her tent, slamming the door behind her.

She rummaged through her closet and found her laptop computer, the same one she'd snuck into camp and had used to help Natalie write her contest-winning essay. Chelsea set the laptop down on her bed and turned it on. While it was warming up, she hooked up her camera to her laptop and uploaded the pictures from her memory card. Once she located a wireless network and hopped online, she created an anonymous e-mail account and transcribed a quick e-mail, then attached the photos from her camera.

To: mail@NationalGazette.com
Subject: Is Camp Walla Walla really "green"?
See for yourself . . .

Chelsea's hands began to shake as soon as she stopped typing. What in heaven's name was she doing? Was she really *that* mad at Natalie?

Tears formed at the corners of Chelsea's eyes, blurring her vision a bit. She knew deep in her heart that she had changed so much since her days at Camp Lakeview. Doing something this mean would be a thousand steps backward for her, and she knew she would regret it.

Chelsea hit the Discard button on the e-mail and sighed in relief. She was happy that she hadn't acted so rashly and stupidly.

After a few deep breaths, she wiped the tears from her eyes with the bottom of her T-shirt and went to turn off her laptop. But when she read what was on the screen, she froze.

YOUR E-MAIL HAS BEEN SENT.

This had to be a mistake. She'd *deleted* it, hadn't she? Chelsea frantically checked the Sent folder and found one item in it. She quickly double-clicked and saw her short e-mail to the *National Gazette*, clear as day.

Chelsea was certain she was going to hyperventilate and then die. Frankly, she was okay with that. At least then she wouldn't have to witness the impact of the fireball that would hit Camp Walla Walla tomorrow when the reporter came.

chapter

TWELVE

Sloan was so nervous by Thursday afternoon, she had nearly bitten her nails down to the skin. Any minute now, Dr. Steve would be bringing the *National Gazette* reporter and photographer to the girls' bunk for a brief interview, and Sloan hoped it would go well.

"Priya, it's my turn to use the mirror," Sarah said, clutching her makeup bag.

"Can't you see that I'm brushing my hair?" Priya replied.

"You've been brushing it for an hour," Jenna teased.

"Quit it, guys," Sloan said, irritated. "We don't want the press to walk in here and see everyone bickering."

"Sorry," Priya said and stepped out of Sarah's way.

"I still can't believe we're going to be in the *National Gazette*," Brynn said brightly. "All my friends back home are going to be so psyched."

Sloan smiled, thinking about how the *Gazette*

readers were going to learn all about the great things Camp Walla Walla was doing these days.

"Has anyone seen Chelsea? I wanted to borrow her tortoiseshell hair clip," Joanna asked.

Sloan was concerned when no one answered. After Chelsea had ducked out of the nature walk yesterday, no one had seen that much of her. Sloan thought it was kind of odd that Chelsea would go missing at a time like this. The interview was about to take place, and Chelsea had an obligation to be there—she was cochair of the Green Committee, after all! A knock at the door interrupted Sloan's thoughts.

"They're here!" Sloan said in an excited whisper. "Everyone act normal, okay?"

"Just not too normal, or else we might scare them," joked Jenna.

Sloan opened the door to the tent and saw a smiling Dr. Steve standing next to a young woman with dark black hair and tanned skin. Behind them was a short, stocky man with a very professional-looking camera in his hands.

"Hello, Sloan. May we come in?" Dr. Steve asked.

"Yes, of course!"

Dr. Steve escorted the *National Gazette* crew into the tent, where all the girls stood in a group, with sincere grins plastered across their faces.

"Ladies, this is Miss Lorraine Gonzales, a reporter with the *Gazette*," Dr. Steve said.

"Hello, Miss Gonzales," the girls said in unison.

Lorraine flashed a beautiful, soft smile. "Nice

to meet all of you."

"And this is her photographer, Lloyd." Dr. Steve pointed to the short, stocky man, who waved hello.

"Thank you again for having us here," Miss Gonzales said to Dr. Steve.

"It's our pleasure," Dr. Steve said. "And I'd love for you to meet Sloan, who is running the planning committee for the Green Festival."

"Welcome to Walla Walla!" Sloan said with enthusiasm as she shook Miss Gonzales's hand.

"We hear that the president's daughter, Tricia, is staying here for the festival. Is that true?" Miss Gonzales asked, looking around the group of girls and trying to spot her.

Sloan swallowed hard. The interview was apparently starting right now!

"Yes, it is," Sloan responded. "But she and another camper are staying in a separate bunk."

"Interesting." Miss Gonzales scribbled something down on a small steno pad, then returned her attention to Sloan.

"I'd really like some time with her," Miss Gonzales said, her soft smile slowly disappearing. "Find out what her experience has been like. You know, big fish in a small pond, that kind of thing."

Sloan glanced at Dr. Steve, whose face was slowly turning pink with what she imagined was anxiety. Sloan could feel her palms getting sweaty, too. She had to redirect this interview with Miss Gonzales so that the Green Festival would get some attention.

"Um, sure. I could set that up," Sloan said.

"But wouldn't you like to hear more about our Green Festival? My friends and I have been working hard to coordinate it."

Miss Gonzales scribbled some more notes. "Actually, Sloan, I do have some questions about that."

Sloan breathed a sigh of relief. "Great. What would you like to know?"

"We received this anonymous tip yesterday." Miss Gonzales reached into her large satchel and pulled out a folder. She opened it and gave Sloan two pieces of paper. "Can you shed some light on this, please?"

Sloan's mouth went dry as she reviewed the contents of the folder. One of the papers was a short e-mail to the *National Gazette*, and the other was a color printout of pictures of a filthy garbage bag filled with nonbiodegradable refuse outside one of Walla Walla's bunks.

"I . . . I don't know what to say," Sloan stammered.

"Isn't it awfully unusual for a camp that's committed to being good to the environment to dispose of its trash in this haphazard fashion?" Miss Gonzales asked.

All the girls started whispering nervously as Sloan stood there, completely still. Lloyd went to take a photo, but Miss Gonzales put her hands on the lens and shook her head.

Dr. Steve took the papers out of Sloan's hands and looked at them worriedly.

Jenna snuck up behind him and glanced over

his shoulder. "Isn't this in front of Natalie and Tricia's bunk?" she gasped. Jenna immediately put her hands over her mouth, like she couldn't believe she had just ratted her friends out.

Miss Gonzales jotted down more notes as Sloan's head began to throb.

"Yes, but this has to be a mistake," Sloan said.

"Sloan's right. Neither Natalie nor Tricia would be so careless," Priya piped up.

"It's true, they're both very conscientious girls," Dr. Steve added.

"Well, why don't we go talk with them?" Miss Gonzales suggested. "I'm sure they can clear this up."

Sloan's body felt like it was melting. "Okay."

Miss Gonzales, Lloyd, Dr. Steve, and Sloan left the bunk and walked silently to Natalie and Tricia's tent. The closer they got, the more Sloan felt like she was going to be sick to her stomach. How could this be happening to her? She had put all her heart and soul into planning the festival, which was only two days away.

Now it seemed as though Miss Gonzales was going to write an article based on this incriminating photo and e-mail and completely ignore all the good she and her fellow campers had been doing. At this point, Sloan just hoped that meeting the president's daughter would make Miss Gonzales forget all about this minor scandal.

When they got to the tent, Sloan was relieved to see that the garbage bag was no longer there. Still, Dr. Steve seemed rather irked when he knocked on the door. Natalie answered it with an unassuming smile.

"Can we have a word with you, Natalie?" Dr. Steve asked.

Natalie appeared to detect the tension in the air and her smile vanished. "Sure. What about?"

Dr. Steve handed Natalie the papers.

"I told them that it was all a mistake. That you and Tricia weren't responsible for this," Sloan said, willing Natalie to agree with her.

Natalie's face went completely white as she looked at the photos. "I . . . um . . . well . . . this isn't a mistake. The trash is mine. I'm sorry."

Sloan couldn't believe it. Natalie was responsible for all of this.

"I wish I could explain right now, but it's all so . . . complicated," Natalie added, her voice wobbly.

Miss Gonzales wrote something in her notebook and then clicked the top of her pen. "Is Tricia here? We'd like to speak with her, too."

"Tricia and one of her security guards took her dog, Paris, to the vet," Natalie explained, her voice wavering. "She came down with a bad case of fleas or something."

Dr. Steve looked at the reporter and her photographer. "Well, why don't we go to my office and talk first," he insisted. "I'm sure we can clear this up in a jiff."

"That's fine," Miss Gonzales replied.

"Natalie, I'll send Jasmine over when we're ready for you, so maybe you could take this time to sort everything out in your mind," he instructed.

Sloan's heart ached as Natalie nodded her head, her lower lip trembling. In fact, Sloan was hurting so much that she couldn't look at Natalie any longer. As Dr. Steve, Miss Gonzales, and Lloyd walked toward his office, Sloan turned and ran away, even though Natalie was calling out to her, asking her not to leave.

▲ ▲ ▲

After Sloan went back to the bunk and explained to her friends what had just happened, she decided to sit under a tree near the lake and watch the CITs teach the younger campers how to dive. She hoped it would relax her and clear her head. As a light breeze swirled around her, she thought about Natalie and what may have possessed her to act this carelessly. Didn't Camp Walla Walla's reputation mean anything to her?

"Mind if I sit with you?"

Sloan looked up and saw Miles towering above her. His eyes were glistening more than the water in the morning sun. Although she was happy to see him, Sloan wasn't sure now was a good time for them to talk.

"I'm kind of in a bad mood, Miles. I don't think I'll be good company," she replied.

Miles sat down next to her anyway and smiled. "I can put up with it."

Sloan laughed a little. "So where are you supposed to be right now?"

"Archery, but Ben sent me to get more arrows," Miles said. "This is just a pit stop."

"I see." Sloan could feel her eyes tearing up, so she quickly turned away.

"Do you want to tell me what's wrong?" Miles asked.

Sloan thought about the second Green Festival meeting and how smart Miles's ideas were. He would probably be able to give her some advice on what to do in this situation.

"Actually, I do. Thanks," Sloan said, slowly turning back to him.

Miles smiled again. "Go ahead."

For the next couple of minutes, Sloan filled him in on the day's scandalous events. Miles sat quietly and listened. When Sloan was finished, his eyes widened, like he'd just heard the camp was closing down or something.

"I just can't believe it. How could she do such a thing?" Sloan said, her voice quaking.

Miles reached over, took her hand in his, and gave it a comforting squeeze. "I have no idea. I mean, I don't know Natalie that well, but she doesn't seem like someone who'd pull something shady like this."

"Yeah, but she's been acting so strange lately," Sloan said, sniffling. "Chelsea has been, too. I guess I just don't know what to think or who to trust."

Miles laced his fingers through Sloan's. "Maybe you should just sit them both down and talk it out."

Sloan really liked how cool Miles's skin felt against hers, and how supportive he was being. She was glad that she had decided to confide in him.

"Natalie tried to get me to hear her out, but I

couldn't. I just ran off," she explained. "Anyway, I'm not sure I'm ready to face her. I'm still pretty mad."

"What are you mad about? That Natalie did something stupid, or that she got caught by a reporter?" Miles asked.

"Well, getting caught wasn't Natalie's fault," Sloan said. "Someone here e-mailed those pictures to the *Gazette*."

"Right. Whoever did that has some major issues."

"But we're never going to know who sent the e-mail. It came from an anonymous account."

"Good point." Miles furrowed his brow.

"I guess I'm most mad about the festival and the camp getting bad press. So many people are going to be hurt by this," Sloan said sadly.

"Do you think there might be a way to get the reporter not to print it?" Miles suggested.

Sloan exhaled deeply. "How are we going to do that? Miss Gonzales doesn't seem easily swayed."

Miles let go of Sloan's hand and stood up. Then he began to pace back and forth, thinking hard. After a minute, he stopped in his tracks. "What if we tell them that the trash bag is only a prop for an anti-litter skit that Natalie is producing for the festival?"

That settles it. Miles is officially boyfriend material.

"I *love* that idea," Sloan said, beaming with joy.

"Why don't I run to the counselor's bunk on my way back to archery and talk with Natalie while you go stall Dr. Steve?"

"He's probably still with Miss Gonzales. I don't

think he'd appreciate me barging in on him."

"You're probably right." Miles paused for a moment. "Why don't you run to the resource center and send him an e-mail? That way it'll pop up on his BlackBerry right away and distract him."

Sloan shook her head. "I'd rather not do that with other people lurking around."

"I see," Miles said.

"Wait a sec. Chelsea snuck her laptop into camp," Sloan remembered.

"Do you think she'll let you use it?" Miles asked.

"She hasn't been around all day, so I'm not sure," Sloan replied. "But I do know where she keeps it."

"This is an emergency. She'll understand," Miles assured her.

Sloan couldn't agree more with Miles. This was an emergency, and besides, Chelsea knew how much the Green Festival meant to her. There was no way she'd get mad over this, given the circumstances.

"Well, we'd better hurry up. We've got no time to lose!" Sloan exclaimed.

chapter THIRTEEN

"So, Natalie, can you explain why all this garbage was found outside yours and Tricia's bunk?" Dr. Steve asked gently.

This was, without a doubt, one of the worst days of Natalie's life. When Natalie had cleaned up Tricia's mess a couple days ago, she had had no idea it would land her and Camp Walla Walla in so much trouble. The only thing Natalie was guilty of was waiting until she could find a golf cart so that she could dispose of the trash bag properly because it had been way too heavy to carry.

However, when Natalie had been shown those incriminating pictures by the *National Gazette* reporter earlier today, she'd known that she couldn't tell the truth about who was the real source of the trash. As one of the most well-known public figures in the country, Tricia's image needed to be protected—Natalie knew this from having a movie star father.

Natalie also knew that in most of her dad's movies, there was a hero that came to the rescue in the end. A short while ago, Miles had shown up at her tent with a masterful plan that he and Sloan had hatched, which was totally going to save her butt.

"Yes, I can," she replied. "You see, I was working on a skit about how littering affects the environment. So I collected all this refuse to use as props."

"What about Tricia? How was she involved?" Miss Gonzales inquired, still not satisfied with Natalie's explanation.

Natalie steeled herself and took a deep breath. "She wasn't. In fact, since I couldn't attend the planning meetings, I figured it would be cool to keep the skit a surprise until the start of the festival. That's why I was kind of secretive when you first asked me."

Dr. Steve beamed with appreciation. He believed this story hook, line, and sinker. "I knew there was a reasonable explanation, Natalie. I'm proud of you."

Natalie wasn't too proud of herself right now. Actually, she felt terrible for accepting Dr. Steve's praise when Sloan was the one who had gotten her out of this mess.

"Can you tell us a bit more about the skit? It sounds like it could be avant-garde," Miss Gonzales said curiously.

Natalie gulped. Apparently she wasn't out of this mess yet—Miles hadn't given her any details beyond what she'd already told them. Still, she was relieved that Miss Gonzales had taken the bait, too.

"Oh, it is. Actually, the skit combines . . . interpretive dance and music wiiiiith . . . performance poetry."

She wanted to smack herself on the forehead. Interpretive dance and performance poetry? It was the most ridiculous thing she'd ever heard.

"Wow, I can't wait to see that!" Dr. Steve practically cheered.

Natalie let out a small sigh. She couldn't wait for the summer to be over.

▲ ▲ ▲

By the time Natalie finally got up the courage to walk into her old bunk later that evening, everyone was so busy getting ready for dinner, they barely noticed her at first.

"Hey, guys," she said apprehensively.

No one made a sound, except for Jenna, who mumbled an awkward "Hi."

Natalie swallowed hard. This was going to be more difficult than she'd thought.

"I wanted to know . . . if it was okay for me to have my old bed back. The mattress in the counselor's bunk is kind of lumpy."

Actually, Natalie was being honest about this. She hadn't been able to get comfortable in bed yesterday and had woken up several times throughout the night.

Priya rolled her eyes and Joanna let out a sarcastic laugh. Jenna looked down at her sneakers, Sarah furrowed her brow, and Brynn's cheeks flushed a dark shade of pink. Chelsea looked as though she might cry.

As she looked at the pained expressions on

her best friends' faces—except for Sloan, who was currently MIA—Natalie realized that she had to tell them the truth about Tricia, regardless of whether it tarnished the girl's image. She couldn't risk losing the friendships she had made at camp. That was asking way too much of her.

After a drawn out silence, Jenna finally spoke up. "Natalie, we just don't understand how you could have been so reckless."

"Guys, if you'll just listen to me, I'll explain everything," Natalie pleaded.

"This better be good," Priya said sharply.

"Yeah, you really let us down, Nat," Sarah added.

Natalie braced herself for what she was about to do.

"I know that I initially admitted that the trash was mine, but . . . I made it up," she began.

"What do you mean?" Brynn asked. "You lied?"

"Yes, I did." Natalie swallowed hard. "But I did it to protect someone. Someone important."

Jenna looked perplexed. "Wait, are you saying that all of that junk was . . . Tricia's?"

Natalie took a deep breath. "That's exactly what I'm saying."

"Wow," said Joanna, her mouth hanging open in shock.

"Tricia kind of has a cleanliness problem, and I've been picking up after her for the past few days," Natalie went on. "I knew I couldn't admit that to the reporters. They'd plaster it all over the place."

Chelsea seemed stunned by this news. She just

stared at Natalie, her eyes glazing over.

After another long, awkward silence, Jenna spoke up again. "Nat, that was a really honorable thing you did," she said, laying a hand on her friend's shoulder.

"We had a hard time believing you'd be that careless from the start," Sarah said.

"I can only imagine how torn you must have felt," said Priya.

It was like a weight had been lifted off Natalie's shoulders. She was glad that she'd told her friends everything. Their support meant so much to her.

"Sloan is going to be very happy to hear this," Joanna said.

"Actually, there's another part of the story that you guys don't know," Natalie remarked.

"Oh, no. Is it bad news?" Brynn asked.

"It's good news," Natalie said with a smile. "Sloan was able to come up with a great excuse for why the trash was outside our bunk. The reporter bought it, so there won't be any scandalous news article to print."

"That's incredible!" Priya said excitedly.

"What was the excuse?" Jenna asked,

"That the trash bags were actually for an anti-littering skit I was doing for the festival," Natalie explained. "And now I have to go through with it, so I'll need some help."

"Count me in, Nat," Joanna volunteered with a smile.

The rest of the girls nodded in agreement.

"Great! But first we have to find Sloan and thank

her for everything," Natalie said.

The sound of the dinner bell echoed through the camp's new energy efficient speaker system, startling everyone for a second.

"Thank god. All this stress is making me hungry!" Jenna joked.

All the girls laughed, except for Chelsea, who looked more sullen than when Natalie had first walked into the tent.

"I bet we'll run into Sloan at the dining hall," Sarah commented.

"Yes, and then everything will go back to normal," Brynn added.

Natalie smiled. She was hopeful that speaking to Sloan would go as smoothly as it had with her other friends.

"Not so fast, guys. We still don't know who took those pictures and sent them to the *Gazette*," Priya said.

"Yeah, that person has a lot to answer for," Joanna agreed.

"Well, we can talk more about it over organic pork chops," Jenna said, licking her lips. "Let's go!"

As the girls filed out of the tent with a spring in their steps, Natalie caught a glimpse of Chelsea over her shoulder. She was sitting on her bed, staring out into space.

"Aren't you going to come with us, Chelse?" Natalie asked.

"No, you go ahead. I'm not feeling so well," Chelsea said.

Natalie remembered how Chelsea had told her how much she'd admired Tricia and how she'd wanted to get to know her so badly. Now that Natalie had revealed that Tricia was far from perfect, Chelsea must be really disappointed. That had to be why she was so sad.

"You want me to take you to see the nurse?" Natalie inquired.

"That's okay. I'm just going to lie down here," Chelsea said with a small smile.

As Natalie left the bunk, she couldn't help but wonder how Tricia would react when she found out that Natalie had revealed the truth about Walla Walla's newest camper.

▲ ▲ ▲

Dinner was a bit of a bust for Natalie. Not only were the pork chops overcooked and tough, but Sloan was nowhere to be found. Natalie even went over to Miles's table and asked him if he knew Sloan's whereabouts, but he was just as clueless as everyone else.

The girls figured Sloan had gone back to the bunk or something—she'd had an exhausting day, after all. Natalie decided to make a visit to Tricia's tent before heading back to her own. She knew she had to fill Tricia in on all that had gone down.

Natalie knocked on the tent door and waved hello to Shepard the bodyguard, who was busy talking with another member of the security team on his push-to-talk phone.

"Come in!" Tricia called out.

Natalie walked in and saw Tricia feeding a Chicken McNugget to her dog. Of course, there were McDonald's bags and Styrofoam all over the floor next to Tricia's bed.

You've got to be kidding me! she thought.

"Hey, Natters! Where have you been?" Tricia said as Paris yelped.

"I was at dinner," Natalie said with a sigh. "How is Paris feeling?"

"She's such a brave girl," Tricia said as she ruffled Paris's fur. "She got a nice medicated bath and is totally flea free."

"That's great," Natalie replied, quite unenthusiastically.

"So why is all your stuff gone?" Tricia said. "I was worried that someone, like, kidnapped you."

Natalie rolled her eyes. Tricia hadn't shown her a lot of consideration since she'd set foot on Camp Walla Walla soil, but the sweet look on her pretty face was going to make it hard for Natalie to tell her that her dirty, nasty garbage habits had almost cost Camp Walla Walla its reputation, and Natalie her friends.

I guess I'll just ease into it.

"Well, I went back to my old bunk," Natalie said. "My mattress there is so much more comfortable."

Tricia gazed at Natalie with skepticism. "Why don't you just tell me the truth?"

"What do you mean?" Natalie replied. "I am telling the truth."

"You're mad at me, aren't you?"

"For what?"

"Wow, Nat, you're a terrible liar. I guess your family's acting gene must have skipped a generation."

Natalie put her hands on her hips. "Excuse me?" she said defensively.

"First of all, I was kidding. Second of all, I'm the one who should be excused, Nat." Tricia's cheery face quickly turned pensive as she continued to pet Paris. "I feel so bad about everything that happened."

"Wait, you know?"

"Yes, Dr. Steve left a message on my cell this afternoon," Tricia said, her voice superserious. "And then Sloan stopped by a little while ago, looking for you."

"Oh, I see," Natalie said.

"I can't believe that you took the rap for me. I also can't believe what a slob I am. I'm not that way on purpose. I just forget. It's something I really need to work on. Anyway, I just can't thank you enough. You're such a good friend."

Although Natalie was touched that Tricia was finally showing some gratitude, Tricia's use of the phrase "friend" made Natalie's head throb, especially after all that she had gone through with her camp friends over this debacle. She had to set the record straight with Tricia here and now. Maybe she'd see the error of her ways.

"Look, Tricia. There a few things I want to say," Natalie began. "I don't really feel like I'm your friend just yet. Actually, I've kind of felt like your personal assistant."

"I'm not following you," Tricia said, perplexed.

Oh boy.

"Okay, um . . . I was supposed to show you around camp as a *friend*," Natalie explained. "But you've been giving me so many things to do, and I've been cleaning up after you so much that—"

"Oh my gosh. Why didn't you say something sooner?" Tricia's eyes widened with surprise.

"I don't know," Natalie said, shrugging. "I suppose I didn't want to hurt your feelings. I really wanted you to like it here."

Tricia's face fell a little and her posture stiffened. "I do like it here, Nat. A lot, in fact."

Natalie grinned. She was happy to hear Tricia say that, regardless of how unbalanced their relationship had been.

"I'm glad," Natalie said. "I mean, I'd like to be friends with you, just as long as it doesn't feel like I work for you. There's a big difference."

Tricia sighed. "You're absolutely right. I guess I'm not used to having *real* friends."

Natalie could feel herself choking up, thinking of how her friends had rallied around her a little while ago. "I felt that way for a long time, too, especially when I first came to camp."

"But now you have lots of cool peeps," Tricia said. "You're very lucky."

Natalie swallowed hard. She had to tell Tricia that her friends knew about her sloppiness, and she had to do it now before she lost her nerve.

"They are really cool," Natalie murmured. "Which is why I had to be honest with them about whose garbage that was."

Tricia stopped petting Paris and froze. "You did?"

Tricia's obvious surprise worried Natalie. "I'm sorry if you're embarrassed or anything. It's just that I couldn't stand my friends being so upset with me, and I didn't want to lose—"

"Fine, I understand," Tricia interjected, her tone somewhat deflated.

"They all promised not to say anything. I know they—"

"I have to take Paris back to the nature hut now," Tricia interrupted again. It was clear as day that Natalie had upset her quite a bit.

There was nothing else she could do but give Tricia some space. So Natalie left the tent quietly, hoping the president's daughter would be more forgiving tomorrow.

chapter FOURTEEN

Later that night, Chelsea lay quietly in her bed as all her friends talked about two very pressing matters: 1) why Sloan still hadn't come back to the bunk; and 2) who took the picture of Tricia's nasty trash heap.

"All I'm saying is, we should think about putting a search party together," Sarah pleaded with her friends as she zipped up her purple fleece hoodie.

"I'm sure Sloan is fine, Sarah," Jenna said. "If she were really missing, Dr. Steve would know by now and everyone would be out looking for her."

"She's probably just neck-deep in Green Festival stuff," Priya said as she closed the last window in the tent and rubbed her arms. There was definitely a chill in the air tonight.

"Yeah, instead we should really focus our energy on trying to figure out who set me and Tricia up," Natalie remarked.

Chelsea pulled the covers over her head, wishing that she'd find some wormhole in her bed that would take her back in time. That way she could warn her other, more idiotic self not to take those dumb pictures and write that stupid e-mail.

Truth be told, Chelsea had been a mess of nerves since she'd accidentally sent that awful e-mail to the *National Gazette*. She felt absolutely horrible about betraying Camp Walla Walla, all because she was both jealous of, and embarrassed by, Natalie. And now that she knew what a good friend Natalie had been to Tricia—how she'd stuck up for her even though it had caused her a lot of pain—Chelsea couldn't possibly feel worse about what she'd done.

"Do you think it could be one of the new campers?" Jenna said. "Maybe it was an initiation dare."

Chelsea's jaw clenched. Hearing her friends attempt to guess the identity of the Camp Walla Walla mole was more than she could bear.

"I don't think so," Brynn said. "No one would suggest a dare that would do so much damage to the camp."

"Yeah, well, whoever it is, I'd really like to give that jerk a piece of my mind," Natalie said, scowling.

"I'm with you. Whoever ratted you and Tricia out to the press was a big traitor," Brynn added.

Chelsea could swear that her tongue was swelling. She just couldn't listen to her friends bash the mystery e-mailer any longer.

"I'm going to the bathroom." Chelsea had never heard her voice sound this downtrodden before. "Be back in a few."

Once Chelsea got to the bathroom, she splashed

some cold water on her face, hoping that would make her feel better. But it didn't help at all. Although she'd been upset at Natalie when she'd written that e-mail, Chelsea would never willingly betray anyone at Camp Walla Walla. If only she could admit what she'd done and plead temporary insanity.

After a few more minutes passed, Chelsea was able to calm herself down enough to return to her bunk. But as soon as she stepped out into the chilly summer air and saw Natalie and Sloan—who was holding Chelsea's laptop—talking outside the tent, she knew she was in for it.

"W-what are you guys talking about?" Chelsea stammered. There was a brief pause, punctuated by Natalie's best death glare.

"I was just telling Sloan who the trash really belonged to."

"Okay, but why do you have my computer?" Chelsea asked, her teeth practically chattering.

Sloan glared at Chelsea. "I borrowed it earlier today to e-mail Dr. Steve."

"You used it without my permission?" Chelsea knew deep down that being confrontational wasn't the greatest idea, but she couldn't help it. Regardless of what she'd done wrong, she kind of felt like her privacy had been violated.

"Well, it was an emergency. Besides, you weren't around to ask," Sloan countered, stone-faced. "Now I know why."

Sloan opened the laptop up so Chelsea could see that in her crazed state she had forgotten to close the Web browser that linked to her now not-so-anonymous e-mail account.

"Guys, let me explain. *Please*. It's not what you think," Chelsea begged.

"How could you do this to us?" Natalie growled, practically spitting nails.

"Just hear me out," Chelsea urged, her eyes watering.

"You hung Camp Walla Walla out to dry, Chelse!" Sloan's voice was just below shouting level. "I've been in a confidential counseling session with Jasmine for hours, trying to figure out what to do."

"It was an accident, I swear. I meant to *delete* the e-mail, not send it. You have to believe me!"

"I can't believe that you even *thought* about doing something like this!" Natalie said sharply. "How deceitful can you be?"

Suddenly, Chelsea's unbearable sadness gave way to bubbling anger. Natalie had some nerve calling Chelsea deceitful! Yes, Chelsea shouldn't have taken those pictures and orchestrated a plot to hurt Natalie—she was so sorry about all of it. But Natalie was acting as though she'd been a *saint* this summer, when she most certainly hadn't!

Chelsea figured it was about time someone reminded her friend about a certain secret they *both* shared. What did she have to lose, now that the cat was out of the bag and everyone was attacking her?

"While we're on the subject, why don't you come clean with Sloan about the essay contest?" Chelsea said, crossing her arms defiantly.

Natalie immediately seemed rattled. Her hands started shaking.

"What is she talking about, Nat?" Sloan asked warily.

"I . . . um—" Natalie couldn't seem to get any more words to squeak through her tight lips.

"Natalie wanted to win that chairperson spot so bad, she had me write her essay for her!" Chelsea blurted out.

"*What?*" Sloan gasped. "You cheated in the essay contest?"

Natalie immediately tried to reason with Sloan. "No, it wasn't cheating exactly. Chelsea offered to help me with the essay, so she interviewed me and kind of ghostwrote it."

"So were you trying to return the favor by blabbing to Tricia that I was her 'biggest fan'?" Chelsea said through gritted teeth. "I can't believe you told her about that Oprah shirt. You promised you wouldn't say anything!"

"Well, excuse me for trying to get you some extra face time with your idol. I guess the rest of Camp Walla Walla and I really *do* deserve to be embarrassed in front of the national media!" Natalie barked.

"Save it!" Sloan snapped. "You are both in the wrong."

Chelsea felt her ears get hot as Sloan stared her and Natalie down. Couldn't she see that Chelsea was genuinely sorry for her mistake? Or that she had a valid reason to be upset with Natalie?

"As far as I'm concerned," Sloan continued, her

voice very strained, "You two owe the whole camp an apology. Until you do that, I'm going to keep a lid on all this so it doesn't destroy camp morale before the festival."

Sloan shoved the laptop into Chelsea's hands and walked into the bunk with her head hung low.

"Happy now?" Natalie asked with an icy stare.

Chelsea's heart was beating like crazy, and she could barely think straight, let alone come up with a good retort. It didn't matter, though. Natalie had already turned around and stormed into the tent.

chapter
FIFTEEN

The sun never shone as brightly as it did that Saturday morning. The temperature was a perfect seventy-two degrees and the air smelled like fresh wildflowers. On a day like this, the grounds at Camp Walla Walla would usually be crowded with kids running from the lake to the archery field to the horse stables. But since today was the opening of the Green Festival, the grounds were also crowded with families from the surrounding area.

As Sloan weaved her way through the crowd, she took in the sights of the festival. There were colorful tents spread out over the main promenade, which were filled to the brim with people of all ages. Sloan walked by a few crafts tents, where Priya and Sarah were checking out the items that the CITs had for sale, like beeswax candles and frames made out of recycled newspaper.

Then she stopped into a couple of the vegetable garden tents, where the counselors and campers were serving up organic food. She caught Jordan and David sampling some ripe red tomatoes and sweet strawberries. Next she visited the entertainment tent, where a bluegrass band made up of a few counselors was playing up-tempo songs that Brynn and Jenna were square-dancing to, in a goofy way, of course.

Sloan wanted to kick back and join in all the revelry—she'd worked so hard in preparation that yesterday went by in a blur—but she just couldn't shake her sour mood. The other day she'd found out that two of her best friends had done some pretty crummy things. Sloan was still baffled by Chelsea's and Natalie's behavior. It was so out of character. Sure, both of them had had their scheming moments in the past, but never when the stakes were as high as this.

How was Sloan supposed to trust either one of them again?

"I must say, Sloan, you did an excellent job," a voice said from behind her.

Sloan turned around and saw Dr. Steve clapping along with the bluegrass music.

"Thanks, Dr. Steve," she said softly.

"I mean it, you should be really proud of what you accomplished here." Dr. Steve tapped his foot with the beat of the drum. "Everyone is having a great time. Isn't that wonderful?"

Sloan let out a long sigh. It *was* wonderful. But she was too bummed out to feel anything but sad.

"I'm happy it turned out so well," she mumbled.

"Are you okay, Sloan?" Dr. Steve asked with concern. "I hope you're not still upset about what happened with the *National Gazette*. Everything worked out. The article that was in the paper yesterday is part of what brought all these folks here."

Sloan forced a small grin. "That's true."

"I'm also looking forward to seeing Natalie's skit," Dr. Steve said, smiling. "It's scheduled for after Tricia's speech, right?"

"Right." Sloan gulped, her small grin vanishing. She hadn't spoken to either Natalie or Chelsea since the other night when she learned about the secrets they'd been hiding. Sloan hoped that Natalie had been working on her skit even though they'd had a falling out.

Sloan glanced down at her watch and then back up at Dr. Steve. "Speaking of Tricia's speech, I have to go meet Miles and Jasmine at the rotunda building. We're helping her practice. We want everything to be perfect before the big event tomorrow night."

"Fantastic! I'm sure she's going to be spectacular," Dr. Steve replied with enthusiasm.

Sloan mustered up another tiny smile and shuffled off toward the rotunda building. She wanted to believe that Tricia could pull off the moving, insightful speech that she and Miles had written, but given the events of two days ago, Sloan wasn't sure if it was safe to believe in anyone, even the president's daughter.

When Sloan arrived at the rotunda building, Miles was standing at the podium, adjusting the microphone. As she looked into his sparkling dark eyes, she felt her mood brighten. Miles glanced up and smiled when he saw Sloan walking down the center aisle.

"*There she iiiiiiis . . . Miss Amer-ic-aaaaaah,*" Miles sang into the mic.

Sloan giggled. "Very funny, Miles."

He turned off the mic and chuckled. "And out of tune, too."

Sloan plopped down in a front row seat and stretched her legs out in front of her.

"Please tell me that Tricia hasn't gone AWOL on us," she said. "I don't think I can take any more drama."

"No, Tricia's just warming up backstage. She should be out in a minute. And Jasmine ran out to get us all some lemonade." Miles sat next to Sloan and nudged her lightly with his shoulder. "How are you holding up?"

"Not well," Sloan admitted, her voice cracking. "I know I should be thrilled with how the Green Festival is going, but honestly, I feel miserable."

"That's understandable. You've been through a lot lately," he said.

"I just wish I could understand why Chelsea and Natalie did what they—"

"Hey, guys," Tricia murmured quietly as she stepped onto the stage and took her place behind the podium, with Jones the bodyguard in tow.

Sloan looked at Miles in bewilderment. This definitely was not the chipper Tricia she had come to know.

"Hi, Tricia. Are you ready to do a dry run-through of the speech while we listen?" Sloan asked, trying to ignore Tricia's melancholy demeanor.

"Okay," Tricia said, casting her eyes down at her feet. "But first I want to say something."

Miles's eyebrows arched curiously. "Sure, go ahead."

Tricia flipped through the pages of the speech. "I'm not sure I want to do this."

Sloan could feel her face flush. Maybe Tricia would rather "talk about her dog" than read this speech, just like Chelsea had warned at their committee meeting.

"Well, we can rework some of the wording if you'd like," Sloan said reassuringly.

"It's not that. The speech is great," Tricia continued. "I don't think I want to do it . . . *at all.*"

Sloan's face went from flushed to crimson red. Tricia's speech was supposed to be the big event at the festival. People from all over town were looking forward to hearing the president's daughter. Sloan could feel a panic attack creeping up at any second.

Miles noticed how anxious Sloan looked and stepped in.

"Sure you do, Tricia," Miles said. "There are lots of folks who are really excited to see you tomorrow."

Tricia stared at the paper on the podium as if she were trying to make the pages disappear with the power of her mind.

Sloan's head was pounding. After all that had gone down with Chelsea and Natalie, she just didn't have the strength or energy to duke it out with anyone else, let alone the First Daughter.

"I don't want to let anybody down, but . . ." Tricia trailed off, her head hanging low.

"Okay, Tricia, you don't have to do the speech if you don't want to," Sloan said. Miles's mouth hung open in shock.

"Thanks, Sloan. I'm sorry about this." Tricia gave Sloan a weak smile.

Sloan just nodded her head, totally resigned.

"What are you doing?" Miles asked her in a whisper.

Sloan merely shrugged as Tricia walked off the stage and out the door with nothing more said than a simple, "See ya."

Miles got up and gaped at Sloan as if he couldn't believe what he'd just witnessed.

"Okay, I'm going to recap the last few minutes, just to make sure I wasn't imagining it," he said. "Tricia just came out here, said she didn't want to do the speech, and then you said it was okay for her to bail. Correct?"

Sloan nodded. "Correct."

"I don't understand," he said. "People are expecting to see her tomorrow. The event was on the flyers and everything."

Sloan's stomach grumbled so loudly that she crossed her arms over it, hoping that would quiet it down. "I know, but what was I supposed to do?"

"Maybe you could have asked her why?" Miles asked.

"What's the point?" Sloan could feel tears forming at the corners of her eyes.

"Well, for one, the Green Festival means so much to you. I thought you might want it to go as you'd planned," Miles said.

"A lot of things haven't gone as planned," Sloan said, putting her face in her hands. "I just feel like I can't count on anyone."

"I think you forgot something," Miles said, his voice gentle and caring.

Sloan looked up from her hands. "What's that?"

"You can count on me." Miles grinned.

Sloan couldn't stop her cheeks from blushing. He was the sweetest guy ever!

"Thanks, Miles," Sloan said. "I feel real lucky to have you as a friend."

"I'm lucky, too," he replied, putting an arm around her shoulder. "Could you just do me one favor?"

"Sure," Sloan said, a hint of a smile inching across her face.

"Keep your pretty chin up," Miles said.

Sloan had to admit, Miles knew just what to say to make her feel better. She also had to admit that she needed to encourage Tricia not to back out of the speech—there was just too much riding on it. But doing so would mean having to talk to someone that she wasn't too fond of at the moment. Nevertheless, Sloan was determined not to throw in the towel.

Not yet, anyway.

chapter SIXTEEN

"Connor, could you hold the Styrofoam container a little bit higher above your head while Joanna and I are reciting the poem?"

Natalie had gathered with a couple of her friends at the rock garden to rehearse her short skit, "Be a Litter Quitter." Their counselor Ellie was helping out with the music and props, which Natalie had rescued from the trash—gross, yes, but also necessary.

"Come on, Nat, we've been practicing forever. My arm is getting tired and I smell like a two-day-old Big Mac," Connor complained.

"Yeah, I don't want to miss the organic corn—grilling contest," Joanna whimpered. "Dr. Steve needs people to root for him."

"This skit has to be perfect, guys, and we're still messing up the end," Natalie said firmly.

"Why don't you try it one more time," Ellie suggested gently. She was standing off to the side watching her campers rehearse.

"Fine," Connor and Joanna muttered in unison.

Natalie smiled, glad that they would have the

chance to perfect the ending. She wanted the skit to be perfect because she was hoping that it would help patch things up between her and Sloan. Natalie sill felt horrible for disappointing her, and she wanted to make things right.

Natalie hadn't seen too much of Chelsea since their blowup outside the tent, which thankfully no one had heard. Sloan had done them both a big favor by not turning them in to Dr. Steve. Even so, Natalie couldn't get over Chelsea's behavior. Accident or no accident, Chelsea could have damaged Camp Walla Walla's reputation for years to come. What Natalie had done wasn't excusable, but it wasn't as bad as that.

"Great, one more time, then," she replied. Then Natalie pointed to Ellie. "Start the music, please."

Ellie pressed play on the portable CD player that they had borrowed from the resource center and a funky beat echoed out from the speakers. Natalie, Joanna, and Connor marched in a line, holding pieces of nonbiodegradable refuse, and prepared to recite a poem that went along with the song. However, just as Natalie was about to dive into the first stanza, the CD started skipping.

"Sorry, Natalie. I'm having some technical difficulties over here," Ellie proclaimed.

Connor stepped out of line and wandered over to Ellie to see what was the matter. He took the CD out of the player and examined it. "Yeah, we've got a problem."

Natalie's shoulders hunched forward in frustration. "What's wrong?"

"There's a scratch on the disc. We're going to need to burn another CD," he explained.

"Does that mean practice is over?" Joanna said, a little too enthusiastically.

Natalie rolled her eyes. "For now, I guess. Let's meet back here in an hour and a half."

"Yay! I'm going to get some grilled corn," Joanna said, sprinting off as fast as she could.

"Me too," said Connor right before he ran after Joanna.

"The skit is good, Nat. Don't worry so much," Ellie reassured her.

"Thanks," Natalie said. She wanted to believe what Ellie was saying, but she had a feeling her counselor was just humoring her.

"I'm going to the resource center to make a new CD," Ellie said. "Why don't you take the props back to your bunk and then join the others at the festival?"

Natalie shrugged. "All right."

Once Ellie left the rock garden, Natalie began to clean up the props and put them in a clean garbage bag. She started thinking about everything that had transpired since the first day of camp. A swell of guilt and unhappiness was building inside of her that she just wasn't sure she'd be able to contain. She'd let Sloan down by taking a shortcut in the essay contest; she'd made Chelsea so upset that she almost endangered Camp Walla Walla's image; she'd even ratted out Tricia so that she wouldn't look bad in front of her friends.

Natalie swallowed hard. Was she the most selfish girl at camp or what?

A voice interrupted her thoughts. "Hey, Nat."

Natalie whipped around and saw Sloan standing with her hands behind her back.

"Hi, Sloan," Natalie mumbled. She was surprised that Sloan had found her here, and that she wasn't at the festival, enjoying all that she had accomplished this past week.

"I just saw a little bit of your skit," Sloan said through a belabored half smile. "I hope you don't mind. Jasmine told me that you were practicing here."

Natalie's stomach churned. Sloan looked as though she was forcing herself to be nice right now, which led Natalie to believe that her friend wasn't ready to make up.

"We still need to work out some of the kinks."

"Actually, I think it's pretty good," Sloan said flatly.

"Thanks," Natalie said. "If it weren't for you, Tricia and I would still be in lots of trouble instead of participating in the festival."

"That's what I came to talk with you about," Sloan said.

Natalie's eyebrows raised in curiosity. "Okay."

"Tricia told me earlier today she doesn't want to do her speech anymore," Sloan explained.

Natalie reeled back in shock. "What? She can't quit the day before her speech."

"Well, she did," Sloan said, sighing.

"Did she say why?"

"No, and I didn't want to pry, so I just told her it was okay if she didn't want to do it."

Natalie's eyes widened. "But . . . what will Dr. Steve say? He's been publicizing this all over town."

Sloan bit her lip nervously. "I didn't think that far ahead. I was just so disappointed that she was backing out on me that I gave in without even trying to convince her."

Natalie felt a little piece of her heart break off. Sloan had been let down so much the past couple of days. This skit wasn't going to be enough to make things up to her, especially after this kind of setback.

"That's why I'm here. I was hoping you could talk to Tricia, since you two are so close and everything," Sloan said.

The rest of Natalie's heart started racing. She was almost sure that Tricia didn't want to give the speech because she was embarrassed about the fast-food garbage heap.

Then another realization came down on Natalie like a thundering rainstorm. She'd argued that she told Tricia about the Oprah shirt because she was trying to help Chelsea. But maybe Natalie had been more concerned with helping *herself*. She'd wanted a break from Tricia so badly that she'd outed Chelsea in the hopes that it would get the president's daughter off her back. In a way, she had done the same thing with Tricia, too—she'd told her friends about Tricia's bad habits to guard her own rep.

"I'd love to help you out, Sloan," Natalie said, her voice wavering a smidge. She needed to get a lot of stuff of her chest, and she hoped Sloan would listen. "But there's something else—"

"Sorry, Nat. I have to get back to the festival," Sloan cut her off, not rudely, but abruptly.

Natalie's stomach tied into a knot. Apparently Sloan wasn't ready to hear what she had to say. "Okay. I'll go find Tricia and talk to her."

"Thanks," Sloan said softly. Then she headed down the trail that led back to the main promenade without looking back.

The other cochairperson of the Green Festival was MIA early Sunday afternoon, the second day of the Festival. Chelsea had graciously volunteered to relieve Holly, one of the junior CITs, of her two-hour shift at the nature hut so she could sing in the Walla Walla folk group. Even though Chelsea wasn't too fond of critters and was sad to be missing some of the festival, it was a good swap for her. Chelsea had been laying super low after her clash with Sloan and Natalie on Thursday night. She knew she couldn't hide forever, but right now, while the three of them were in the midst of a cold war, she was better off staying on the sidelines.

As Chelsea fed the turtles and fish in their brand-new energy efficient aquariums, she tried to sort out all the conflicting feelings in her heart. On the one hand, she felt awful for breaking Natalie's confidence about the essay out of pure spite, and for being jealous of how well Natalie and Tricia were getting along. On the other hand, Chelsea still felt like Natalie had wronged her and that she deserved some kind of payback. The only person who was innocent in all this was poor Sloan. It would probably be a while before she could trust either Chelsea or Natalie again.

A series of high-pitched barks shook Chelsea out of her thoughts. She wandered over where the rabbit cages were lined up and saw Tricia's precious Cavadoodle panting inside a large, mesh crate. Chelsea saw that the dog's water bottle was nearly empty, so she refilled it from the tap. She took a quick moment to ruffle Paris's fur and smiled.

"At least you're not mad at me," Chelsea muttered.

But as soon as Chelsea closed the door to the crate, Paris started barking again.

"Maybe I spoke too soon."

Chelsea peeked at Paris's dog food bowl and observed that there was plenty of puppy chow in it. Then she checked out the newspaper lining the mesh crate, which was totally clean. Eventually she put two and two together and decided that Paris most likely wanted to go out for a walk. But since there was no one else to keep watch of the place, Chelsea figured that it was best to just loop Paris around the hut a few times.

"Okay, okay. I'm getting your leash, hold on," she said to Paris, who continued to yelp.

Chelsea took the dog's hot pink leash off a hook on the wall and opened the door to Paris's crate.

"Are you ready to get some exercise, girl?"

But before Chelsea could attach Paris's leash to her collar, the door flew open. It was Holly, back from her stint on the festival circuit.

"Hey, Chelsea, you doing okay?" she asked.

Before Chelsea could answer, Paris leaped from her cage and bolted right past Holly and out the door.

"Paris! No!" Chelsea yelled as she watched the dog sprint away.

Holly was beside herself. "I'm so sorry!"

But Chelsea didn't have time to calm Holly down. She had to chase after Paris and catch her before she got lost. If she didn't find her, she would be even higher up on Tricia's hate list!

Chelsea pumped her legs and arms harder than she had on the day of the canoe race. She jumped over stray logs and through bushes, keeping Paris in her sights at all times. But no matter how fast she ran, Paris was always a few steps ahead of her.

What are they putting in her dog food, anyway?!

It wasn't long before Chelsea realized that Paris was headed straight for the promenade, where the Green Festival was being held. She needed to nab her before she got lost in the crowd, or even worse, hurt herself. Tricia would never forgive Chelsea if something bad happened to her precious dog!

But try as she might, Chelsea couldn't snatch Paris up in time and watched helplessly as she ran underneath the large banner that read WELCOME TO CAMP WALLA WALLA'S GREEN FESTIVAL and into the large crowd of festival-goers.

"Watch out! Coming through!" Chelsea shouted as Paris wove in between the legs of unsuspecting adults and children.

Her heart beating one hundred miles a minute, Chelsea kept up the mad dash, even when she had to push through a crowd of locals who were eating grilled corn on the cob.

"Excuse me! Pardon me!" she yelled, tailing Paris as she darted below picnic tables.

Chelsea nearly collided headfirst with Dr. Steve, who she noticed was wearing a blue ribbon on his vest for some reason.

"Chelsea? What on earth are you up to?" he called after her.

"Can't talk now!" Chelsea screamed back at him.

Paris made a quick beeline for the hill at the end of the promenade, and Chelsea didn't slow her pace, even though she was exhausted. Her leg muscles ached as she followed Paris up the hill and down a trail that led to the low-ropes course. Chelsea felt cramps form at both her sides, and she was certain she'd have to quit if they didn't go away.

Luckily for her, Paris stopped in her tracks once she came to the horse stables, which were located at the bottom of the hill. As Chelsea caught her breath at the top, she looked down and saw Paris licking the face of her owner, Tricia, who was flanked by her bodyguard, Shepard.

Chelsea descended the hill slowly, wiping the sweat off her forehead with the sleeve of her T-shirt. She was nervous to approach Tricia looking like a mess, but frankly, her joy that Paris had stopped running outweighed any self-consciousness she felt.

"Poochie! What are you doing out here?" Tricia cooed to as she scratched her dog under its neck.

"I'm sorry, she got away from me just when I was about to take her for a walk," Chelsea said with a timid smile.

Tricia laughed. "She's done that to me plenty of times. Thankfully, Shepard is an expert dog catcher."

Chelsea chuckled a bit, and so did Shepard, who apparently had had his fair share of dog pursuits.

"How come you're not at the Green Festival?" Chelsea asked Tricia. Her big speech was coming up in a few short hours.

"I'm kind of hiding out here with Shepard," Tricia said, still petting Paris lovingly. "What about you?"

"I'm doing the same thing," Chelsea said, sighing. "I would have been nice and safe in the nature hut if Paris wasn't such a rascal."

Tricia smiled at Paris as she wagged her tail frantically, but Chelsea could see that Tricia seemed rather wistful.

"I hope you don't mind me asking, but why are you hiding?"

Tricia took a deep breath and exhaled. "You know why."

Chelsea wracked her brain, but couldn't figure it out. "I don't think I do."

"Natalie told me that she revealed my not-so-little dirty secret . . . *literally*," Tricia said with a half grin. "There's no need to pretend that you haven't heard."

Chelsea was surprised at Tricia's reaction. It was true that Natalie had told everyone about Tricia's bag of trash and problem with keeping her space clean, but Chelsea had been so involved in her own problems and the Green Festival that she hadn't given it a second thought. She was pretty sure the rest of the girls felt the same way.

"Honestly, Tricia, Natalie mentioned it just to clear up a misunderstanding, but I had forgotten all about it." Chelsea squatted down next to Paris and patted her affectionately on the head.

"Really?" Tricia said.

"Yeah, and I'm sure everyone else has, too," Chelsea continued. "Everyone is just so excited that you're here and that you're going to speak today at the festival."

Tricia looked down at her sneakers. "Actually, I'm not going to do the speech today."

"That's too bad," Chelsea said sympathetically. "I know a lot of people were looking forward to it."

"But there are a lot of people there who probably think I'm America's biggest slob now. And I bet Natalie thinks that I'm a spoiled brat. It just hurts because I felt like I was really starting to make friends here," Tricia confided.

"Listen, Tricia, that's all water under the bridge. No one is going to judge you for it. I can honestly say that you are genuinely well-liked here," Chelsea said with a sincere, warm smile. "Even by Natalie."

"You're not just saying that, are you?" Tricia asked.

Chelsea giggled a bit. "Would your biggest fan ever lie to you?" It suddenly occurred to Chelsea how easy it was to talk to Tricia when she wasn't thinking of her as a celebrity, or an idol, or a potential BFF. If only she had been able to do that sooner.

Tricia let out a huge laugh. "I said it before and I'll say it again. We just need to follow each other around 24/7!"

Chelsea was so relieved that she and Tricia were hitting it off. Sometimes friendships evolved out of the strangest of circumstances.

"I don't know about that. I have to admit, I was so embarrassed when Natalie told you about the dreaded Oprah shirt," Chelsea said, her cheeks flushing the lightest shade of pink.

"First of all, I heart that shirt," Tricia said, her sassy tone back and better than ever. "Second of all, I had forgotten all about that, too."

Chelsea threw her head back and practically guffawed. All of her worrying was over nothing. "Gee, I'm so glad that I didn't stress about that or anything," she said sarcastically.

Tricia joined in the laughter and Paris let out a few cheerful yelps. "So, do you feel like sitting backstage and watching a big speech?"

Chelsea smiled in gratitude, but decided to decline. "I think I'd rather sit in the front row. With all your other friends."

▲ ▲ ▲

About two hours later, the eco-friendly rotunda building was buzzing. All of Camp Walla Walla plus an additional hundred people were gathered together to listen to the president's daughter talk about what kids across the country were doing for the environment. There was a hum of excitement in the air as campers and members of the surrounding community whispered to each other, wondering what Tricia was going to say.

No one was more excited than Chelsea.

"I'm so glad we got front row seats," Priya said happily. "Aren't you, Chelse?"

Chelsea smiled with enthusiasm. "Yeah, this is great."

"I wonder why Tricia's speech hasn't started yet," Jenna said, checking her watch.

"Yeah, the flyer said that Tricia was supposed to speak at five," Brynn said.

"She's probably just running late." Chelsea's stomach lurched a little bit. What if Tricia had changed her mind and decided not to go through with it?

"Has anyone seen Sloan? I saved her a seat," Jordan said, tapping the seat next to him.

"I think she and Miles are helping Dr. Steve," said David.

Priya craned her neck around and squinted out into the crowd. "Oh, wait. There she is in back."

Chelsea turned and saw Sloan standing in the far back of the room, glancing around nervously. Her heart fluttered with anxiety. What if Sloan and Natalie never forgave her?

"I'll get her attention!" Sarah knelt on her seat and waved both her arms in the air.

"You look ridiculous," Brynn said.

Sarah ignored Brynn's comment and kept on waving. Chelsea kept her focus on Sloan, who shook her head and mouthed the words, "Not now," when she caught Sarah's eye.

Chelsea swallowed hard.

She probably doesn't want to sit here because of me.

"Huh, that's really weird," Sarah said, sitting back down in her seat. "If she's not hanging out with Miles and Dr. Steve, then why doesn't she want to sit with us?"

Chelsea contemplated getting up and leaving so that Sloan could join the rest of their friends. Sloan had been nice enough to ask Chelsea to cochair the Green Festival committee, and how had Chelsea repaid her? By accidentally sending an incriminating e-mail to the *National Gazette*. If the shoe were on the other foot, Chelsea would still be pretty angry, too.

"I wonder where Natalie is," Jenna remarked.

"Yeah, I didn't think she'd miss Tricia's big moment," added Brynn.

Jasmine leaned over from the row behind them and said, "She's with Ellie, Connor, and Joanna, doing a little last-minute practicing for their skit."

Another big pang of guilt tweaked Chelsea's heart. It was her fault Natalie was scrambling around, preparing for a skit and missing Tricia's event.

Forget about Sloan and Natalie never forgiving her. As the clock kept ticking, Chelsea wondered if she'd ever forgive herself.

chapter

EIGHTEEN

Sloan ducked backstage after she scanned the crowd for Natalie and Tricia. She was *thisclose* to falling apart. The rotunda building was packed and Tricia's big speech was already supposed to start ten minutes ago.

"Any sign of them out there?" Miles asked, his forehead wrinkled with worry.

"No." Sloan was ninety percent certain she was about to throw up. "Where's Dr. Steve?"

"I told him the mic wasn't working, so he stepped out for a sec to find another one," Miles replied.

"Good thinking," Sloan said, wringing her hands. "I swear, I'm about to freak out, Miles."

"It'll go fine," he said, patting her on the back.

Easy for you to say, she thought. *I'm one heartbeat away from cardiac failure!*

Thankfully, Sloan didn't die on the spot, or throw up. Instead, she breathed a deep sigh of relief when Natalie showed up. Now they could finally get on with the show.

"I'm *so* glad you're here," Sloan said, her pulse slowing down to a dull roar. "Where's Tricia?"

"I don't know. I've searched everywhere and I couldn't find her." Natalie's voice was tinged with anxiety.

Sloan cradled her head in her hands. "What are we going to do?" she groaned.

"I don't know. I'm so sorry, Sloan," Natalie replied quietly.

Sloan hung her head and covered her eyes with her hands. This was turning into a huge disaster.

"Uh...um...I guess I could deliver the speech."

Sloan wiped a stray tear from her cheek and looked up at Miles, who was smiling sweetly at her.

"I can't promise that I won't stink at it, but I'll try my best," he added.

Sloan just couldn't get over how supportive Miles was, and how willing he was to help others. She hadn't thought she could like him more than she did, but she'd just been proven wrong.

"That won't be necessary, chicas!"

Sloan swiveled her head around and spotted Tricia, looking prettier than ever. She had her hair back in a sleek, low ponytail and was wearing a beautiful— and familiar-looking—blue shirt. Her makeup was soft, yet done in a way that made her eyes really pop.

"Tricia, thank God!" Sloan said, deliriously happy.

"Where have you been? I've been searching high and low for you," Natalie said.

Tricia suddenly looked a bit bashful. "Good ol' Shep and I, like, took a teensy staycation at the horse stables. I was feeling kind of lousy. But then—"

Sloan wanted to hear more of Tricia's story, but

they were behind schedule and she could tell by the murmuring on the other side of the curtain that the audience was getting restless.

"Tricia, we have to get you onstage right away," Sloan cut in urgently.

"Okay, you got it, girlfriend," Tricia said without missing a beat.

Sloan exhaled deeply. She was beyond relieved now that Tricia was here. Sloan almost didn't even care what she said to the crowd, as long as she said the word "environment" just once.

All of a sudden, the stage curtain opened and Dr. Steve stepped through.

"I fixed the mic, Miles," he said, brushing his hands together. "You're up."

A curious look came over Sloan's face as Miles walked onto the stage.

What's going on?

Sloan, Natalie, and Tricia watched from backstage as Dr. Steve dimmed the houselights. A hush fell over the audience. Then a faint spotlight fixed on Miles, who was standing at the podium.

"Hi, everyone. Thanks for coming to the Green Festival," Miles said, his voice shaking a bit. "I just wanted to offer a special thanks to the person who made today possible. She did a great job of organizing this event and keeping everyone in line."

A collective chuckle emitted from the audience.

"I'd like to ask Sloan to come onstage and be recognized," Miles said cheerily.

Sloan had to admit, she was full-on smitten

with Miles at the moment. When she came onstage, she gave Miles a big hug as her friends in the front row whistled and cheered. Then she made her way to the podium. Sloan briefly locked eyes with Chelsea, who was cheering harder than anyone, but then she glanced to the back of the room just as swiftly.

Stay focused, she told herself.

"Thank you, Miles," Sloan said into the microphone. "Chairing the planning committee was both fun and challenging. I hope you enjoy the rest of the festival. Camp Walla Walla really appreciates your support."

The audience applauded and Dr. Steve took her place at the podium. Sloan returned backstage to watch with Natalie and Miles.

"Now, without further ado, please welcome our keynote speaker. It has been a privilege to have her here with us, and we know her father would be proud of her," Dr. Steve said, his voice lilting. "Ladies and gentleman, the First Daughter of the United States!"

The crowd erupted into a fit of cheers and feverish clapping when Tricia appeared onstage, looking like a trillion dollars.

"Thank you for the warm welcome, everyone. And special thanks to you, Dr. Steve, for all the work you and the people at Camp Walla Walla have done for the environment," Tricia said with perfect diction.

Sloan still couldn't get over how Tricia could turn this presidential persona of hers on and off. It was unbelievable.

"Today I was supposed to give a speech about what kids across the country are doing to protect the natural resources of our planet." Tricia's eyes scanned the audience, making a connection with everyone in the room. "And while it's an important topic, I'm afraid that there is something just as pressing that I need to address."

Sloan's ears perked up. What was Tricia about to say?

"Would Natalie Goode come join me onstage?"

Everyone in the crowd started to whisper. But Sloan couldn't bring herself to say anything— she stood there completely dumbstruck, helpless as Natalie approached Tricia from backstage.

"Natalie was asked to be my special guide here at Walla Walla, and she took her job very seriously, making sure to show me around and explain every- thing there is to know about the camp," Tricia said.

Sloan thought back to the day that Dr. Steve had asked Natalie to step down as committee chair- person so that she could help Tricia. While Sloan was still pretty perturbed at Natalie for really bending the rules in the essay writing contest, she couldn't help but think how nice Natalie had been to give up something that meant a lot to her so that she could make Tricia feel welcome. Didn't that outweigh the sneaky thing she'd done?

"Well, I'm not proud to admit this, but up until now, I didn't take being here or at the Green Festival very seriously at all," Tricia continued. "In fact, Natalie took responsibility for a mistake that I made so that the camp's image and my good standing among you all wouldn't be damaged."

"Wow, can you believe this?" Miles murmured to Sloan.

Sloan was completely stunned, and so was the rest of the crowd, if their whispers were any indication. To be honest, Sloan hadn't given Natalie enough credit for telling the *Gazette* reporter that the trash heap was hers. And if Miles hadn't come up with his great damage control plan, Natalie probably would have had to shoulder all the blame.

"So I'd like to offer a sincere apology to Natalie," Tricia said, extending her hand out to Natalie. "And ask her and her friends for forgiveness."

Natalie shook Tricia's hand firmly and then tiptoed off as the audience clapped. As the applause died down and Natalie took her place backstage, Sloan turned and gazed at her friend. After hearing Tricia graciously apologize, she realized that she was definitely being too hard on Natalie. However, when Sloan glanced at the front of the room and saw Chelsea, her stomach rumbled. She just couldn't let her anger at Chelsea go, and wasn't exactly sure that she should.

Tricia pushed forward with her remarks.

"Making that apology felt really good," Tricia said. "Actually, I don't think I've felt this good in a long time. You see, I've traveled all around the globe, and while those experiences were extraordinary, there was one thing missing—friendship.

"If you think about it, friendship is the most organic, green thing on earth. The kinder and gentler and friendlier we are to Mother Nature, the more she gives to us, as well as to future generations," Tricia went on.

Sloan couldn't be more thrilled with how well Tricia was doing. So far, her impromptu speech was way better than what Sloan and Miles had written.

"The opposite can be true, too. When we take our relationship with the environment for granted and severely neglect it, our world breaks down, little by little," Tricia said captivatingly. "I don't want to wake up one day to find that there's nothing left. Do you?"

Sloan wiped a tear from her eye. To her, Tricia's speech seemed to have a whole other meaning altogether—Sloan didn't want to wake up and find her friendships with Natalie and Chelsea were gone forever, regardless of what may have happened between them.

"So if we haven't been good friends to Mother Nature in the past, we should forgive ourselves and start being good friends now." Tricia paused for a moment and smiled. "And that's what I plan to do here, at Camp Walla Walla."

Sloan scratched her head, wondering what Tricia meant by that.

"Being here has shown me the power of friendship, especially today. In the spirit of honesty, I have to admit something else—I came close to ditching this speech because I was worried about what some of the campers thought of me. But a friend talked some sense into me, and then gave me this gorgeous shirt to wear."

All of the audience members who knew about the Oprah shirt debacle laughed—and Chelsea laughed the hardest.

"So thanks, Chelsea, for being both a fan and a friend," Tricia said. "I really appreciate it."

Sloan's brain nearly caved in. Chelsea was the one who got Tricia to reconsider making the speech? She was so touched by Chelsea's gesture. Obviously, her friend had a big heart. In the grand scheme of things, didn't that matter more than the mistake Chelsea had made?

"With all that said, long, lasting friendships are something that I really want in my life. So with my father's permission, I will be staying at Camp Walla Walla for the rest of the summer," Tricia said with a smile.

The audience cheered so loudly, they nearly blew the solar-paneled roof of the building. Sloan grinned when she saw the entire first row stand up and applaud. No one could be happier about Tricia's announcement.

As Sloan listened to the remainder of Tricia's speech, she felt like a huge weight had been lifted off her shoulders. Tricia's words about forgiveness and the power of friendship really resonated with her. However, Sloan would have to put everything to the test in a few minutes when Tricia stepped offstage.

"I'd like to close with a quote from Walt Whitman, which Natalie told me came by way of our friend Chelsea, for whom she is very grateful," Tricia said with a smile. "Give me the splendid silent sun with all his beams full-dazzling."

Sloan was surprised once again. Tricia was doing everything she could to patch things up between her,

Natalie, and Chelsea. Sloan was definitely grateful for that.

"Let's go out into the sunbeams and enjoy the day," Tricia concluded. "Thank you all so much!"

After a standing ovation and final round of applause, most of the crowd filed out of the building and outside to experience the rest of the Green Festival. The front row, however, stayed behind and assembled around Tricia, congratulating her on a job well done. Sloan slowly walked down the center aisle, hoping that Chelsea and Natalie were as affected by Tricia's speech as she was.

"Seriously, I was two seconds away from sobbing like I did at the end of the Hannah Montana movie," Priya said to Tricia.

"You actually paid money to see that?" Joanna asked.

"It's not her fault. I dragged her there," Sarah admitted.

"She dragged me, too. It wasn't so bad," Jordan said.

Everyone laughed but Chelsea. After the high of Tricia's speech, Chelsea's mood had dropped again, and Sloan could tell just how sad she was from a few feet away.

"Is it safe for us to come out now?" Miles was standing off to the side of the stage, behind a red curtain. Next to him was a wary-looking Natalie.

"You betcha," Tricia said, her feisty voice returning as the last adult exited the room.

As Miles and Natalie walked over, everyone

started clapping, a sight that Sloan was very happy to see.

Suddenly Chelsea piped up. "Nat, I've got something I have to say to you."

Sloan held her breath. Chelsea wasn't going to ruin their chances at reuniting, was she?

"I am so so sorry for how I treated you. I hate to admit this in front of everyone, but I was jealous of Natalie for getting to hang out with Tricia and, well, for others things, too. Can you forgive me, Nat?"

Natalie's lower lip trembled. "I'm sorry, too, Chelse. I should have been more sensitive to your feelings and honored my promise to you."

Then both Chelsea and Natalie turned toward Sloan, their faces remorseful.

"Sloan, I think we hurt you the most," Chelsea said, her voice quivering.

"It's true, we both let you down big-time," Natalie said in agreement. "Do you think you could find it in your heart to—"

Sloan couldn't contain her emotions any longer. "Stop it! You guys are breaking my heart!"

She pushed through the group and wrapped both Chelsea and Natalie in a three-way hug. The rest of their friends all seemed very befuddled.

"Um, did I miss something?" Brynn asked.

Jordan shook his head. "Yeah, what are you guys going on about?"

Tricia laughed. "Trust me, this story is juicier than anything you'd see on TMZ."

"Really? Well then, you'd better start dishing,"

Joanna said with interest.

"Joanna's taste for gossip is insatiable, Tricia," Sarah warned.

"Speaking of taste, can we do this over Dr. Steve's winning organic corn on the cob? I'm starving," Miles said.

Sloan smiled at Miles and playfully linked arms with him. "I'm hungry, too."

"Great, let's go find some chow!" Tricia said enthusiastically. "But first we have to head to the rock garden to watch Natalie's skit."

"Oh joy," Connor said.

"Come on, Connor. Don't you want everyone to see your awesome rap skills?" Natalie said while giving him a huge pat on the back. "Besides, it'll be over before you know it."

Everyone chuckled at Natalie's joke as they filed out of the rotunda building, one by one down the center aisle. That is, except for Natalie and Chelsea, who walked together with their arms around each other.

Miles copied them and put his arm around Sloan. "May I?" he asked with a grin.

"Definitely," Sloan grinned.

Once they got outside and into the sun, that beautiful Walt Whitman quote echoed in Sloan's mind. After a great day at the festival with all her friends, Sloan had forgotten the exact words. But the sentiment of the quote—and Tricia's speech—was sure to stay in her heart all summer long.

Here's a sneak preview of

camp CONFIDENTIAL

TOPSY-TURVY

available soon!

chapter ONE

Priya woke up with a huge smile on her face. All night, she'd dreamed about Ben—having dinner with Ben, holding hands with Ben, chatting with Ben under the stars. She didn't know much about him yet, but in her dreams they'd had a *ton* in common. And even though Priya knew those had just been dreams, she couldn't deny that she just had a great *feeling* about this guy.

When she got into the bathroom to wash up, though, she suddenly felt confused. There was hardly anyone in there. At the sink stood Natalie, brushing her teeth, but she was still wearing her cute pink gingham pajamas. She paused, spit, and washed off her brush, then ran her hands under the water and tried to slick back her pillow-mussed hair.

"Hey, Priya," Nat greeted her. "What do you have your clothes on for? Remember, it's Opposite Day."

Priya groaned. She couldn't help it. Upside Down Day was supposed to be fun, but she'd woken up with plans to "dress to impress" a certain boy camper. This was about the *last* day she would ever want to wear pajamas to breakfast. She looked down at herself: She was wearing a holey T-shirt from her basketball championships and a baggy pair of boxers with little goldfish all over them.

Nat smiled at her. "Gee, you look disappointed," she said, a spark of understanding in her eyes. "Does that have anything to do with a certain cute boy I heard you asking questions about last night?"

Priya felt her face flush. She wasn't used to having crushes, and the idea of sharing this one felt a little scary, like it might lead to public humiliation. "Uh . . . um . . ." she stammered.

But Nat just looked sympathetic and patted her on the shoulder. "No worries, Priya," she assured her. "Jenna told me you were asking about Ben. And I think it's *awesome* you like him; you two will make such a cute couple!"

Priya smiled. She had to admit, it made her feel good that Nat had said *will*—"you two *will* make such a cute couple"—almost like it was a done deal!

But then she remembered Upside Down Day and groaned. "The thing is," she told Nat, "I was going to dress all cute today, and I forgot we have to wear our pajamas for Upside Down Day. *Now* what? I don't even have cute pajamas."

Nat glanced at the cubbies, where all their clothes and accessories were stored. "Hold on," she whispered, then darted around Priya to her cubby. She grabbed a couple frilly, flowery pieces, then ran back to her friend. "Here, this is my extra set—how about you borrow these?"

Priya took the pajamas from Nat and looked them over. They were beautiful—a delicate flowered cami with eyelet lace accents, and a pair of purple silk pants. *Nat's pajamas are more fashionable than half my* outfits, she thought. But she couldn't deny that they seemed perfect for attracting boy attention, on a day when not many campers would be looking cute. "Are you sure?" she asked Nat. "You don't mind me borrowing them?"

Nat shook her head. "Come on. This is camp. What's mine is yours. Besides," she leaned in and whispered, "Priya, you never crush on anyone. You're so busy running around with Jordan, sometimes I wonder if you even *notice* other boys. I think you totally deserve to have a camp romance. And seriously, you and Ben would be great together. You should go after him."

Go after him. Priya wasn't entirely sure what that meant, but whatever it was, she almost felt ready.

"No problem."

Once Priya was dressed up in Nat's fancy pj's, Nat helped her create the perfect "just rolled out of bed looking amazing" hairstyle, and even helped apply some pink-tinted lip balm to "give your lips a little glow." Then she loaned Priya a pair of sparkly flip-flops—"Slippers would be too *obvious* with that ensemble," Nat warned—and a delicate pink cardigan to wear over the cami, in case she got chilly.

"Awesome." Nat grinned, looking over her handiwork. "You look like a million bucks!"

Suddenly, someone behind Priya yawned super-loudly. Priya turned to find Brynn, wearing an old pair of gym shorts with a hoodie and rubbing her eyes. "Wow, look at you, Priya," Brynn muttered, taking in the full *look*. "You don't usually sleep this super-fancy, do you?"

Priya bit her lip. She wasn't sure she wanted everyone to know that Nat was helping her dress up to win a boy's attention. But Nat just deflected Brynn's questions with a shrug. "I loaned Priya my pj's last night because she got toothpaste on hers," she said breezily. "It's no big deal."